W9-BVL-839

The Heirs of Locksley

ALSO BY CARRIE VAUGHN

The Ghosts of Sherwood
Bannerless
The Wild Dead
Discord's Apple
After the Golden Age
Dreams of the Golden Age
Voices of Dragons
Martians Abroad
Steel
The Immortal Conquistador
Amaryllis and Other Stories (short stories)
Straying from the Path (short stories)

THE KITTY NORVILLE SERIES
Kitty and the Midnight Hour
Kitty Goes to Washington
Kitty Takes a Holiday
Kitty and the Silver Bullet
Kitty and the Dead Man's Hand
Kitty Raises Hell
Kitty's House of Horrors

The Heirs of Locksley

Carrie Vaughn

A TOM DOHERTY ASSOCIATES BOOK

NEW YORK

This is a work of fiction. All of the characters, organizations, and events portrayed in this novella are either products of the author's imagination or are used fictitiously.

THE HEIRS OF LOCKSLEY

Copyright © 2020 by Carrie Vaughn

All rights reserved.

Cover art and design by Liz Dresner

Edited by Lee Harris

A Tor.com Book
Published by Tom Doherty Associates
120 Broadway
New York, NY 10271

www.tor.com

Tor® is a registered trademark of
Macmillan Publishing Group, LLC.

ISBN 978-1-250-75661-9 (ebook)
ISBN 978-1-250-75662-6 (trade paperback)

First Edition: 2020

For Claude and Basil

MARY OF LOCKSLEY WAS not important enough to have a very good view of the coronation, but she had a better view than most, halfway down the nave in the church at Westminster. So much finery, so much gold, blinding wealth and pomp, a great stone hall full of arches and pillars and a soaring timber roof. The cathedral at Canterbury was larger, she'd been told, but she wasn't sure she believed it. In the center of it all, the king, surrounded by bishops and councilors and all the great lords of England. Mary's father was only a baron and one of the former rebel barons at that, so she stood with the rest of the crowd to look on. Eleanor, her youngest sibling, stood on her toes trying to see until their mother put a hand on her shoulder and she settled. John, the middle child, stood shoulder to shoulder with their father.

John had turned more serious these last couple of years. The recent war had come almost to their doorstep. Many of the rebel barons had supported the French invasion in an attempt to depose King John. For once, their father hadn't picked sides—he hated King John, but a French king wouldn't have been any better, he insisted.

For a time, they thought they would have to fortify Locksley Manor against one army or the other. Then, in the middle of it all, King John died.

"How is it possible I outlive him?" Robin of Locksley had murmured when the news reached them. The two had been enemies all their lives, yet somehow the news of the king's death had made Robin sad. Mary hadn't understood.

"He can't hurt you now," Lady Marian had reassured him.

"Oh, but he can," Robin answered with a harsh laugh. "We'll see what the son is like."

The war had ended, the invasion had been thwarted, and a second, formal coronation was held to establish the young king's rightful place on the throne. King Henry III was now thirteen years old, thin and somber, overwhelmed by the azure mantle on his shoulders and gleaming crown that the Archbishop of Canterbury settled on his head and straight reddish hair, neatly trimmed. His voice was small as he made his oaths, but unwavering, serious. So serious. He never once smiled.

"He's so young," murmured Marian. "I knew he was young, but to see it. I want to feed him biscuits and make sure he has a warm cloak."

Robin smiled and hushed her.

Despite a thought that she should pay close attention

so she could tell the story of this to her children, assuming she ever had any, Mary's attention kept wandering to the attendant gathering, the lords and ladies of England, looking for a young man of about the right age, but since she had no idea what he looked like, she couldn't know if he was here.

Then it was all finished and the gathering broke apart, the sea of people pushing back toward the doors. The councilors and great men clustered around the king, who vanished behind a sea of finely dyed wool and glittering trim.

"Is William de Ros here?" she asked her father, trying not to sound too interested. Merely curious. Casually curious.

"No, I don't think so. The de Roses must have been delayed," Robin said. Mary blew out a sigh. "Don't worry, you'll get to meet young William this time. In just a few days, I'm sure."

He'd been saying that for years, since she was sixteen. She was twenty now. William de Ros was the man her father wanted her to marry. Hoped she would marry. Something. She had said she would agree to it if she liked him, but she would have to meet him first. Not that she knew how to tell whether she would like him or not. Did it even matter? She would have to marry *someone,* wouldn't she? She simply wanted to be able to decide, one way or another.

It was all very frustrating, like walking a dark forest path with no idea of the destination.

Marian touched her shoulder. "Mary, will you take Eleanor outside? The crowd is too much, I think."

Her sister's gaze was downcast and she rubbed her fingers together as if she spun wool, but she'd left her spindle behind and so had nothing but the movement. It was a sign she was getting nervous and unhappy. She'd been fascinated with the proceedings right up until she wasn't, when the ritual and ceremony, and thus the order of it all, ended. Mary offered her hand, which her sister took with both her own. The elder sister made herself a shield to push through the crowd until they reached the side of the church, which had fewer people, and from there they could flee out the transept doors. Some of the clergy gathered there raised their eyebrows at them, but they moved quickly and with purpose and no one stopped them. Besides, one veiled woman looked much like another. They could pretend they were nuns.

Suddenly, they emerged to sunlight, fresh air, and relative quiet. Mary hadn't realized her own shoulders ached from holding herself so formally for so long.

"Well then, is that better?"

Eleanor sighed and leaned into Mary, but she still would not look up and went back to rubbing her hands nervously.

On this side of the church, an herb garden and walk-way led to the cloisters. Beyond the church, moving away from the confluence of the Rivers Thames and Tyburn, was the palace and village of Westminster, where a great fair had sprung up as an excuse to celebrate the coronation. Musicians played, acrobats performed, women sold mulled wine and meat pies from carts. The day had been full of ceremony for the high-born, but for everyone else it was a festival. And a bit further down the river, London, with all its noise and bustle, tall buildings and tangles of streets, and so many people. There was no escaping the people. They'd have to go miles to find a forest.

It was all so different from home.

She found a low garden wall to sit on while they waited for the others. Finally, Eleanor was herself enough to look up.

"I suppose being left at home would have been harder for you than coming here and putting up with all this," Mary said absently. "I'm not sure I like it. It's well enough to visit a town, but I miss Sherwood." Eleanor nodded. She never spoke, not a word. People ignored her, discounted her, thought her stupid. But Mary was sure that her sister saw everything, noticed everything. Sometimes, she'd give much to know what Eleanor was thinking. She looked over the abbey garden behind them. "You might like a convent. No crowds, little noise." Eleanor wrinkled her nose and shook her head. Not very pious, that one, but the priest who heard their confessions assured them that though she could not speak, he could tell that Eleanor was contrite and so absolved her of whatever sins a thirteen-year-old girl might commit.

God must take special care to look after one such as Eleanor; Mary was sure of it.

A commotion rose up at the transept door, and there emerged onto the path a crowd of liveried attendants, pages with cups and cloaks, bishops with their mitres, dukes and lords with collars of state, and in the middle of them all a tall, thin boy. All processed this way. Mary quickly tugged Eleanor to her feet. "Here, curtsey now, hurry."

As the king and his company passed by, Mary curtseyed deep, her face down. Kept her arm across Eleanor's shoulders to make sure she did likewise. She did steal one quick glance. Eleanor was doing just the same, curiosity getting the better of both of them, though they'd have done better to go unnoticed.

In that moment King Henry looked over, caught her gaze. She nearly choked. What was the penalty for accidentally looking at the king? Well, nothing for it but to smile—so Mary offered a quick smile. King Henry smiled back, just as quick, before turning his attention to the path as his lords and bishops marched him onward, back to the sprawling palace.

"Well, what about that?" Mary said, after the commotion had passed by and she and Eleanor straightened to look after it. Eleanor was smiling, which meant she liked the boy king. Eleanor didn't like many people. Like as not, though, that was as close as any of them would get to him their whole lives. That was a story to tell her children.

~

Moments like this, John knew all the old stories about Robin the outlaw were true. Even now, his father behaved like a man who had lived with a sword at his throat for years. He kept his back to the wall, and when there wasn't a wall or a good solid oak to shelter by, he never settled.

"Where are they?" Robin said, keeping to the edge of the festival crowd. He searched his surroundings with a focused manner that was disconcerting, as if he expected a fight to break out and needed to predict where the first blow would come from.

"I sent them out the side door. Eleanor needed air," Marian answered. She took Robin's arm, and it wasn't for herself; it was to steady him.

"Ah," Robin said, and continued to search for enemies.

"There they are," Marian announced and went off to meet the two figures walking arm in arm from the church. Their veils fluttered, their skirts rippled. Mary was a woman grown, John was startled to see, though honestly she had always seemed old and staid to him. She was taller than their mother, otherwise almost her picture, with dark chestnut hair braided up and a bright face. Eleanor would be their triplet in a few more years, though her hair was light. John wondered what he looked like, standing next to his father. Still a foolish lanky boy, no doubt, his coat too big and his shoes too small. He had no beard to speak of yet.

John started to go with his mother, when Robin called to him. "A word, John."

Robin turned all that intense attention on his son, and John felt the weight of it though he tried very hard to not show it. He was aware of steeling his shoulders so they would not seem to bend. *To be this man's heir . . .*

"Yes, sir?" John said.

His father put a hand on his shoulder. "When the time comes, you will go swear fealty to the king on my behalf, as my heir."

"I will? But . . . why?"

"Did you notice?" Robin of Locksley said. "The young king is surrounded by old men. His father's men, old councilors and bishops. Until he comes of age, they're the ones ruling the kingdom. The king—he will need friends close to his own age. And you will need to get to know him. God willing, you will be dealing with each other as liege lord and vassal for decades to come. All those old men—and me—will be dead sooner rather than later. King Henry will need friends. Do you understand?"

To his own shock, John thought he did, and this worried him. He was used to not understanding much of anything beyond which end of a sword or arrow was meant to go into the enemy. But maybe that applied here after all, in a manner of speaking. "This is about politics."

"Yes. And about a young boy who looks as if he could use a friend or two. Your sisters will go with you. You'll all make a pretty picture, I wager. It should catch his attention. I'm not asking you to scheme or plot. Just . . . be his friend, if it turns out he wants one."

"Yes, sir. I understand, I think."

"Besides, I would only be a distraction." He grinned and winked. Ah yes, the old king's men would remember Robin, wouldn't they?

"You want Mary along so she'll kick me in the ankle when I say something stupid," John said.

Robin laughed. "You see, my lad, you know exactly what you're about." He ruffled his son's hair—had to reach up to do that; John had gotten that tall, at least.

It wasn't facing the king, pledging fealty, or the formality that gave John pause. It was all the old men around the king, as Robin had said. They would not take John seriously. He had done nothing to prove himself. He had nothing to recommend himself, except for who his father was.

He did not like this talk of Robin being gone one day. Then all would fall to John.

"What's this?" Robin murmured.

A group of men approached. The one in the lead, a solidly built man with a trimmed brown beard and glaring eyes, older than John but not nearly as old as Robin, was richly dressed, a red mantle over an embroidered coat, with gold clasps, a fine leather belt and shoes. With him were a handful of knights and squires, swords at their belts and steel in their gazes.

Robin glanced across the square, gave a bare nod. His oldest friend, Will Scarlet, was there, a tall silver-haired man in plain tunic, unassuming by intention. He leaned up against the corner of a shop, supposedly watching a juggler. He nodded back but stayed where he was, alert, unobtrusive.

John wasn't as good with heraldry and faces as Mary was. Who was this man?

"My lord Pembroke," Robin said expansively as the

man stopped a few paces away.

"My lord Locksley," he replied evenly. He and all his men glared. John watched even more eagerly now—the second earl of Pembroke, William Marshal, the son of the famous William Marshal. This was the man who had probably ordered the kidnapping of John and his sisters four-odd years earlier. He had thought to win favor by taking hostages that would ensure Robin of Locksley's compliance during the baronial rebellions. Robin had sent back the would-be kidnappers with arrows in their throats. There had been some to-do over the deaths; the young William Marshal had denied any involvement in the plot, but enough of a question on that score was raised that no murder charges had been brought against Robin. Either both of them had committed mortal insult, or neither of them had, and that was that, and now here they were.

"I was very sorry to hear of your father's passing, my lord," Robin said. "We will not see his like again."

The younger William Marshal seemed unconvinced, studying Robin with a frown. "Thank you. This is your son?" His gaze shifted, giving the boy a skeptical look.

"This is John, yes."

"My lord," John said politely. And because he couldn't resist: "I understand we missed a chance to meet several years ago." If the kidnappers had succeeded, he and the girls would have been delivered to this man's feet. John was glad to be taller now than he had been, to look the man in the eye, or close to it.

Pembroke's gaze narrowed. "It's just as well. These are . . . happier days for such a meeting."

"Indeed," Robin said, and gave his son a sidelong glance. "Let's hope they remain so."

"A good day to you, my lord." Pembroke inclined his head and turned to leave. Each of his men seemed determined to glare extra hard at Robin, as if that would affect him at all.

"And you!" Robin called after them.

"Is he going to cause trouble?" John asked.

Robin shook his head. "I think any trouble with him died with the old king. But watch your back."

Will Scarlet sauntered over. "It's always the really well-dressed ones with the sourest looks, isn't it?"

"We are all loyal subjects of the king," Robin murmured. "I will just keep telling myself that."

John had the sudden thought that his father's pushing him into this world was akin to being thrown to wolves. He really ought to learn to keep his mouth shut better if he was going to manage.

~

Rather than follow Robin and John back to camp, Mary and Eleanor went with their mother on an errand. She led them confidently around the church, past the abbey, and to a set of timber-frame buildings clustered together behind their own wall. One could see the high stone bell tower of a chapel beyond, and the thatched roofs of houses and outbuildings. Mary gave her mother a confused look. Eleanor's look was even more confused, growing apprehensive, and she held back. There had been some talk of Eleanor taking vows, but nothing serious, and Mary didn't think their mother would simply . . . *deposit* her at a convent without discussion.

"Don't worry," Marian told them with a happy smile. Open and honest, unlike her circumspect, diplomatic manner. "I'm visiting an old friend."

An ironbound door marked the entrance. Marian knocked, and a coifed and veiled woman answered. "I'm here to see Mother Ursula, please. It's Lady Marian."

"Yes, my lady, please come in."

The door opened, and the three of them entered the grounds.

The convent's front yard was a place of refuge and charity, filled with the poor and crippled and struggling, gaunt of face and dressed in rags, crutches tucked under arms. Eyes bandaged, limbs missing. Suffering. Mary's first response was to draw back, look away. Eleanor took her hand and squeezed. It was helplessness, not disgust, that made her want to turn away. At Locksley, they could take in their own people, help them as they needed. But here in town, so close to London, there were so many . . .

A bustling woman, plump and energetic, wearing a nun's dark habit, wooden cross swinging on her chest, came into the yard. With all the fabric around her face, judging her age was difficult, but Mary guessed that Mother Ursula was close to Marian's age.

"Mother Abbess," Marian said warmly, holding out her hands, which the abbess clasped.

"Marian, how wonderful to see you!"

They embraced. Yes, old friends.

"You don't look a bit older, do you?" the abbess said.

"I certainly feel older. I've brought a small offering. Just a bit to help." She drew a pouch from her sleeve, pressed it into Ursula's hands.

"Bless you, my dear. We will put this to good use and say prayers for you and yours." Her gaze turned to study the girls. "These are your daughters?"

"Mary and Eleanor. I have a boy in the middle. He's with his father."

"His father," she said wryly, with a lift in her brow that told just what she thought of their father. Mary hid a smile. "And what mischief is Lord Robin about these days?"

"None at all," Marian declared with perhaps too much force. "There has been too much trouble these last few years. We are hoping for calm."

Ursula said, "With a boy king and so many men of power hunting around him like foxes?" She shook her head with apparent disgust. "He is a poor king, at present. We will see what he does to get money, and how much like his father he is. Though I hear that he is pious, at least."

Mary's heart went out to the young king. That one could never hear of him without hearing of his father, to grow up under a famous shadow . . . She understood this. Robin, at least, was not so universally hated as King John had been.

Ursula waved off the serious discussion. "You are fine-looking girls, aren't you? Oh, Marian, how far we've all come!"

Mother Ursula showed them what parts of the convent she could. The chapel, of which she was very proud, and the gardens, which were bright and full of budding spring flowers. She and Marian chatted the whole time, gossiping about people Mary had never heard of. The abbey was much quieter than the town—the wall setting it apart made a difference, but it was more than that. Everyone seemed to move slower here. Even Eleanor seemed calmer.

"Are you married yet, child?" Mother Ursula asked over her shoulder at the girls.

How Mary hated that question. "Not yet, Mother," Mary said, trying to mirror Marian's easy, proper manners.

"Soon, perhaps," Marian said smoothly, diplomatically. "We've got our eye on someone."

Bloody William de Ros, why couldn't he simply show himself?

She turned back to Marian. "If either of your girls decides that their paths lie with God, I hope you'll send them to me."

"Of course," Marian said. Eleanor wrinkled her nose. Mother Ursula laughed.

On leaving, Marian and Ursula embraced again, clasped hands, and made promises not to wait so long between visits. The abbess kissed Mary and Eleanor on their cheeks, said a blessing over them, and then they were back to the world of noise and chaos and sin.

Marian explained, as they walked on. "We were at court together when we were young. She's the daughter of an earl and didn't much care for the idea of being married off as a political maneuver. Since she had plenty of sisters, she went to the convent instead. It suits her. It may not seem like a large realm, but she has power over it. She's doing good work here, and that was all she wanted, to be able to do some good in the world, and not be a pawn." Did Marian sound wistful?

"Did you ever think of the convent?" Mary asked.

"I did, but only when it was an alternative to marrying someone loathsome. Then your father came along." Her gaze held a merry glint.

One of their father's men, who had been an outlaw with him years before, had been waiting outside and fell into step behind them. He had been watching them unobtrusively the whole errand, right up to the convent doors. Just in case.

"All is well, Dav?" Marian asked.

"It is, my lady. No trouble."

"It's when we don't expect it that trouble comes along, hm?" she observed, and Dav merely smiled. "So today, at least, all is well."

Eleanor clasped Mary's arm, and Mary kissed her little sister's head. All was well, at least for now.

~

The king called his barons and knights to swear fealty before the week was out. John half-expected his father to change his mind, to deal with the young king himself. But he didn't, so he, Mary, and Eleanor arrived at the grand hall where Henry held court, dressed in their best and attempting to behave like they knew what they were doing. The place was crowded, thick with the smell of candles and sweat, and everyone looking over everyone else in a calculating way that made John's spine twitch. Who was in favor, who wasn't, and how the balance of power would shift in the years to come. How did one ever learn to read it all?

John was now very glad that their mother had been so insistent that they learn French. It was the only language anyone spoke here, except for the occasional Latin. He already felt at a disadvantage, not knowing anyone. But at least he understood what they were saying.

Mary was also studying the assemblage with a narrowed gaze and thoughtful frown.

"Are you still looking for William de Ros?" John asked.

She winced unhappily. "Is he here, do you think?"

"I don't know why you bother when you don't even know what he looks like."

"His family arms are red with water bags on it. Maybe he's wearing his arms."

John's brow furrowed. "Heraldic water bags? What does that even look like? No lions or leaping stags or—"

"Never mind." How was it she was the most nervous of them all? It wasn't like she'd have to actually speak to the king. Even Eleanor seemed settled, holding on to Mary's arm and glancing around with wide, interested eyes.

A herald called names. Lords approached and knelt before the king. Oaths were exchanged. Each meeting took only a minute or so. John ought to be remembering the names, as he realized he could not recall a single one he'd heard in the last ten minutes. Lady Marian would say he should mark each one and learn what he could about them, in case he needed the information later. Their mother was much better at court politics than all the rest of them put together; *she* should be the one here—

And then there was only one name before theirs. He squared his shoulders. This would be simple; all would be well. "Here we are. He'll hardly notice us and this will all be over."

"Are you well?" Mary asked their sister, who let go of her hand and clutched her skirt, standing up straight and proper. Her lips were locked in a tight line but she nodded. All these crowds, all these strangers, she must hate this, but she was being very brave. John tried to smile encouragingly but she was focused on the way ahead and did not see him.

Then it was their turn. "Lord John of Locksley, with Lady Mary and Lady Eleanor," the herald announced.

The three siblings stood before King Henry.

His chair was too large for him, and he gripped the ends of the arms as if he expected it to tip over. He sat rigidly, with determination. How this must be trying his patience. At his age, John had only wanted to ride and shoot and practice swordplay. Did King Henry ever do anything but sit in chairs and look serious?

"My liege," John said, and knelt at the place on the carpet that was scuffed from dozens of other knees. Behind him, he sensed Mary and Eleanor curtseying so deeply, they nearly touched the floor—they had spent the morning practicing. He had been paying enough attention to know what would follow: one of the bishops would tell him what he was swearing to, loyalty and tribute and all the rest. John would swear, the king would promise to follow the law and protect his servants, and then it would be over.

Instead, a young voice interrupted.

"Lord John of Locksley?" The king leaned forward in the great chair, curious, demanding.

The hall fell silent. Everyone was staring at him. Absolutely everyone. John's heartbeat seemed very loud all of the sudden.

"Yes, Your Grace," he said, making his voice clear. His French had an accent that was out of place in this court. He was so obviously English.

"Your father is Robin of Locksley?" King Henry asked. Several of his councilors murmured among themselves and looked discomfited. They remembered that name well.

"Yes, Your Grace." He rather thought he knew what came next. The question was always the same.

"Do you know archery?" Suddenly Henry was very much a boy, not a king.

John smiled. He couldn't not. This was familiar ground. He spoke to the boy, not the king. "I do. My father taught me."

Henry's eyes lit up. Much murmuring gossip among the courtiers answered this, as he knew it would. Everyone knew the stories about his father.

The king had a boyish smile to go with the smooth face and bright eyes. "We should like to see you shoot sometime."

John was surprised to note that he also spoke French with an English accent.

"At your pleasure. But . . ." He glanced behind him. His sister would not thank him for this, even if he only spoke the truth. "I do not shoot so well as my sister, Lady Mary. Of all of us, she truly inherited my father's gift."

"A lady archer!" Henry exclaimed. "Is it true?"

Now all eyes were on Mary, and he could almost see her repressing the urge to throttle him, instead donning her most polite manners. She couldn't be surprised that John threw her forward like this . . .

"My brother flatters me, Your Grace," she said properly, elegantly. "But yes, I do shoot."

"You will show us, yes?"

"At your pleasure, Your Grace," she answered. Oh, John would catch hell from her later.

King Henry had bent the ear of the nearest councilor to him, a middle-aged bishop in a black coat, with dark eyes and a glaring manner. The councilor nodded, then King Henry did.

He announced, "We will hold an archery contest. A simple affair, all in fun, on the tournament grounds. Tomorrow. We will see you there, and anyone of our court who wishes to test themselves against you, and see who is the best."

"Of course, Your Grace," Mary said, curtseying even lower somehow. King Henry grinned happily.

"Sire, the oaths," one of the other bishops put in. They had almost forgotten the business at hand. So, oaths of fealty were exchanged, and finally a steward gestured the three of them away.

They left the royal chamber and emerged in the hall outside, where the swarm of courtiers and attendants and hangers-on gathered, with much drinking and eating and talking and watching and scheming, and it was all just noise. Mary stopped and looked heavenward. Eleanor stood between them, grinning. She approved, at least.

"Aren't you going to yell at me?" John asked. "Tell me that was the stupidest thing I've ever done, to draw the king's attention like that—"

Mary started walking again. "On the contrary, I think Mother and Father will be most impressed at how you found a way to curry favor. I'm rather impressed myself."

Well, that hadn't been the reason at all; he'd only wanted to see if the boy would smile—"Then you don't mind me throwing you into this?"

"I don't mind shooting before the king. But the way everyone stared at me like I'm some kind of . . . a trained dancing bear!"

"People like dancing bears," he offered.

"John!"

"We can't escape Father's reputation. We might as well use it, yes?"

"Well, then, if we're going to shoot in a contest tomorrow, we'd best hurry home and check our bows."

At least she'd stopped searching the crowd for William de Ros.

⁓

Once, four years earlier, Mary made an impossible shot, at dusk, in the forest, a hundred paces away from a line-thin target using a bad bow and worse arrow, her nose bleeding from where their kidnapper had struck her. She made the shot, just to spite the brute.

She had only gotten better since. But practicing archery was usually what she did to avoid people, not put herself in the center of the entire kingdom's attention. She decided she might as well make a spectacle of it, so when it came time to dress for the match, she wore a kirtle of Lincoln green.

"Well," her mother said when she saw. "You'll leave them no doubt whose child you are."

"I have given up arguing over it," she answered. "And if William de Ros is there, best he know what he'll be getting right up front."

"Perhaps you should stop worrying so much about William de Ros."

"Truly, I'm no longer sure he exists."

"Oh, Mary. Have patience."

The travelers who had come to Westminster for the coronation filled all the inns and manors and beds in town, so many of those there to pay homage spilled out into encampments in the countryside. It seemed a second town had sprung up, the companies of dozens of England's knights and lords clustered in tents and pavilions, carts and wagons. The baron of Locksley camped apart from the others, near a sparse woodland of undersized alders, closest thing to a forest for miles around but it would have to do.

The whole company gathered to see them off. A good

number of the Locksley stewards and tenants had been outlaws with Robin, back in the time of King Richard. They still kept watch over each other, as if they could not get out of the habit. The only ones missing were Brother Tuck, who had died when Eleanor was a baby, and Little John, who did not like to come out of Sherwood's shadow for anything. Mary had grown up in that circle of safety and protection and trust—she was only starting to realize what that meant, to have a whole troop at one's back. One could stand up to an awful lot of trouble.

That she would have to leave the company, perhaps soon, was a thing she hadn't much considered.

"The green suits you, Mary," Robin said, coming up from the back of the camp.

"Will you not come and watch?" she asked.

"I fear I would make you nervous if I did."

She thought a moment. "It might, yes. I'm sorry."

He came up and straightened a corner of her veil. "Never mind. I've seen you shoot plenty of times and will do again."

When John appeared, pulling a quiver over his shoulder, he was also dressed in Lincoln green, a belted tunic with brown leggings. A matched set, like they planned it this way. Mary slipped her own quiver over her shoulder, adjusting her veil around the strap. Will Scarlet, who served as the Locksley household's steward, had looked over their arrows personally the night before and reassured her that she knew what she was about and had nothing to prove. She picked up her bow, as yet unstrung, from the nearby rack.

"Well, look at you both," Marian said, touching her fingers to her chin. "You have your arm guards? All your arrows counted? Extra bowstrings, you should have extra strings—"

"Mother, we've checked everything three times over, we're fine," John said.

"My lady, they will do very well," Robin said, taking Marian's hand.

Now she looked like she was about to cry. "I am so very proud of you both."

Mary kissed her mother on the cheek and offered a smile. "It will all be over soon one way or another."

"Be easy, Mary, just this once," Marian said.

"Yes, my lady."

"Ready?" John asked her. She nodded and they set off, with the whole of the Locksley household looking after them. The weight of the regard was heavy. John, her little brother who was taller than she was now and had somehow started the barest shadow of a beard growing and seemed so terribly sure of himself, said, "She's right, there's nothing to worry about. We're telling a story, that's all."

"The story of Robin Hood? Are we supposed to be play-acting, then?"

"Yes, in a sense."

Eleanor met them on the path into town, standing expectantly, hands clasped before her. She had a spindle and roving tucked in her belt, her veil was neat, she didn't look at all out of place except that she wasn't supposed to be here. She was supposed to be back at camp, with Beatrice and their mother.

Mary sighed. "We talked about this. You shouldn't come. It'll be loud and crowded and—"

Her sister tipped up her chin and marched ahead.

"I'm not going to argue with her," John said, shrugging, and followed her.

And how was it that Eleanor managed to get her way so often when she didn't even speak? This was going to be a long day, Mary feared.

The royal household had put together as fine an archery pitch as Mary could imagine. A dozen butts spread out along the distant end of the field, newly painted, the target colors bright. The stands were filled with the same rich and varied collection of lords and ladies as at the coronation, pages and attendants, banners fluttering over shaded viewing stands. All so pretty and lively. Were they supposed to bring attendants? Tables and chairs, silver platters full of food and drink?

No, never mind, they were here to shoot.

"There," John said, looking over the gathering with a calculating eye. "There is the king, and I wager that's his archery master." A collection of men with bows and quivers had gathered on the ground near the middle of the viewing stand, where the largest of the banners flew, and the richest lords and ladies sat. In the middle of them all, a boy sat formally in an ornately carved chair. The king.

The archery master, an older man wearing a baldric of royal red and gold, moved among them, taking names and looking at bows.

"They're all men," Mary said. "I know I'm not the only woman in England who shoots. I thought . . . well." She didn't know what she thought.

"It may only be that they're not here today," John said.

He was sweet for trying to make her feel better.

If Mary hoped they could slip in unnoticed, and that there would be a whole crowd of archers to lose herself among, she hoped in vain. Mary and her siblings appeared, and the crowd turned to watch. Maybe the green wasn't such a good idea after all . . .

"Trained bear," she muttered.

"Don't forget to smile," John said, touching his cap.

Eleanor hesitated, bumping into Mary and clutching her skirt. Mary wanted to hiss that she'd warned her it would be like this, but she didn't.

"Can you find a quiet place to sit?" Mary asked. Preferably someplace no one would try to talk to her . . . Eleanor bit her lip and nodded. Gave Mary a quick kiss on the cheek for luck, which was heartening, and then she ran off to a spot on the grass near the end of the viewing stand, where some other young girls sat with sewing and spinning, that still had a good view of the field.

A dozen men had come to shoot in the king's contest. They looked over when the Locksley siblings approached, their gazes narrowed and appraising, their lips frowning or smirking. *We must look like such children to them,* Mary thought.

Her bow felt like an old friend, holding her hand.

"Lord John! Lady Mary! Welcome!" the king called.

John bowed deeply. "Your Grace, thank you for the opportunity to display our meager talents for you."

The chair, the ermine, the gold, the fluttering banners, all of it would make one forget this was an eager boy grinning back at them. *We're telling a story,* John had said. And the king wanted a story. Well, then.

She smiled, just like John asked, and kept her gaze down as she strung her bow and adjusted her arm guard. Let them stare; she didn't need to stare back.

The king came out to address the archers and the crowd. He looked back at his councilors, and the same dark-robed bishop who was always with him nodded encouragingly. There was an odd sense that this was a child playing at being king.

But then his young voice, right on the edge of cracking, announced with determination, "For the winner, we have a gold ring from our own treasury!" He held up the ring, a gold band with a dark stone. There was cheering. Mary didn't think of the ring, only of getting through this with her dignity intact.

"Archers, take your marks!"

Mary leaned close to John as they chose targets next to one another. "Promise me you will shoot your best and not throw the match because you think it's funny to have people stare at me."

"Mary, I promise you with all my honor that I always shoot my best against you. You really are that good. You're as good as Father."

She wasn't. She could never be. The very fundamental definition of their father—at least in the stories—was his skill in archery. "We never saw him in his prime, when he was young and fighting the sheriff's men in Sherwood. Do you ever think of that?"

He turned pensive. "No."

"We will never be that good, not ever. I have never split an arrow."

"Then perhaps today's the day for it."

Perhaps.

"Lady Mary, you do not use a longbow like your father?" The question came from the archer on her left, Ranulf FitzHugh, the son of a baron from Essex.

She looked up and down the line. Of the dozen men who'd come to shoot, two used Welsh-style longbows, including FitzHugh himself. Not even John used a longbow for this, though he could have.

"No need to, my lord," she answered. "I'm not shooting deer or sniping at Normans from two hundred paces, am I?"

He chuckled nervously.

John added, "Think you the targets will escape if you don't strike them hard enough, my lord Ranulf?"

Flustered, he said, "The use of the longbow requires special skill—"

"Yes, it does," John said. "But you must remember, it doesn't matter how deep your shaft plunges if you can't find your mark!"

This was met with general, raucous laughter. Except from Ranulf, who turned away scowling.

"Really, John," Mary chastised, and this too was met with laughter. "You drag us any lower, we'll need a shovel to get out of the mire."

"You let her talk to you that way?" a man from the viewing stand called to John.

He called back, "If you don't have an older sister, you'll

never understand! They're supposed to harangue their little brothers!"

With just a couple of quips and a ready laugh, John won over the crowd. Even the somber bishop smiled. Mary just had to follow his lead. She checked the crowd, found Eleanor sitting quietly, alert and interested. So, all was well there. John gave her an encouraging nod, which she returned.

"Archers ready!" the master of the field called.

Finally, she could be with herself, ignoring the other archers, the crowd, the king. Bow and arrow and target. This she knew. She wet a fingertip, raised it to the air, which was still, mostly. She nocked her arrow and drew.

~

Those who watched King Henry's coronation archery tournament thought it was a joke at first, the two fresh-faced archers from Nottinghamshire acting like Robin Hood's heirs, making jokes about shooting Normans—they glanced nervously at the king for guidance, wondering if they should laugh or be offended. It must have been a joke. Robin Hood was only a story.

The boy was good; all could tell he knew his way with the bow, had likely been shooting all his life. But the girl was the only one to hit the target dead center. Then she did it again, and again. It seemed at first she must have split her own arrow—just like in the stories. But no, the latest arrow only shaved off some of the shaft of the previous.

"Waste of a good arrow," she muttered, when the page brought her arrows back and she studied the scarred shaft.

She seemed a quiet young woman, tall and lovely, and those among the spectators who knew her mother agreed that she was very like her, if not as refined. That came from growing up in the northern wilds, away from civilizing influences.

They shot a second set. Lady Mary once again made a tight cluster of arrows. The archery master cleared out half the archers, ordered the targets moved back. The two Locksley siblings remained, along with the surly man with the longbow, Ranulf FitzHugh, who kept glaring at the young lady.

As they lined up, fingers on bowstrings, Ranulf shouted with sudden temper, "You should not be here! It's an insult!"

Likely, this was meant to make her flinch—the stewards and spectators nearby did. But she didn't. She let out the tension in her bowstring and stared at him. Just stared, until he looked away.

"Switch places with me, Mary," John murmured.

"It's all right," she replied. "Can't let a little wind bother me, can I?"

Ranulf shot badly that round. When the archery master culled the field again, he was cut. So was the Locksley boy. He didn't seem to mind. Only three archers remained.

The king called Lord John to him. The young man knelt at Henry's feet.

"How does she do it?" Henry asked him.

One might have expected the son of Robin Hood to spin a tale, to say it was magic, their father's spirit, the hand of God, some mysterious quality that only came from drinking the water of the springs that bubbled up in Sherwood Forest. He said nothing like this.

"Watch, sire. You see, she stands solid. Nothing wavers. When she aims, the aim stays true. She moves the same every time, drawing to exactly the same point on her chin. Her feet never shift. Now see Master Gilbert there. He's very good, but he isn't so consistent. He doesn't hold himself still. His hips swing, his shoulders buckle. He stands a little different each time, so he cannot make his arrows stay true. This might be enough for him to hit a broad target, bring down a stag if there's no wind. He's a willow, and Mary is an oak." John would never admit his pride of Mary to her outright, but he would brag to anyone, outside her hearing.

"I see it," Henry said, wonderingly. "Have you just revealed to me the secret of Robin Hood's shooting?"

John chuckled. "The secret is practice, nothing more. Anyone could tell you that."

"She's very good."

Mary had just released her sixth arrow this round, and John held his breath, hoping this one would split one of the others. But no. It merely tore off some of the previous arrow's fletching. That would annoy her.

"She once said that the sap of Sherwood Forest runs in the marrow of our bones. I think she's right."

A few of those there, one or two of the older barons and their attendants, a couple of grizzled foresters who had come away from their northern woodlands, had once watched a different archery contest and couldn't help but make comparisons. The girl's father had been flashier, but this one—this one was steadier. If she were a boy, they might wish her for their own guard. Put her on the wall in a siege, no one would get past her.

Ranulf kept calling out, shouting insults that grew harder to ignore. John watched the man closely, and when he picked up a small stone, hefting it as if meaning to throw it, he could no longer keep still.

"I beg your pardon, sire. I must leave you for a moment." He didn't wait for permission, which he should have done if he was being proper, but there wasn't time. He went over and grabbed Ranulf's wrist. The man was so startled, the stone dropped from his hand. "Can't stand to have her win, is that it? Or are you so shamed at being outshot by a woman that you must hurt her?"

"What—"

He ought to call the man out. Draw swords, run him through right here for being churlish and unchivalrous and simply awful. But that would start something John likely couldn't finish. That would be fighting this man on his own ground.

"Never mind," John said, and donned a sly grin. "Shame fades in time." He patted the man's cheek, just shy of a slap.

"How dare you—" Ranulf batted away John's arm and swung a punch. John managed to duck and drew back to drive a blow of his own in the man's belly, but he was grabbed and hauled back. The king's guards had intervened, two of them holding fast to John, two to Ranulf, keeping them apart. Gathered courtiers watched tensely, maybe even eagerly. John straightened and tried to look as contrite as possible.

"All is well," he murmured. "I apologize for the outburst."

Ranulf jerked himself from the guards' grasps, and the crowd sighed. At a signal from the tall bishop in black, the guards stepped away. John kept a space between them, waiting to see what the other would do next. After a last glare, Ranulf made a quick bow to the king and stormed away.

"Lord John, I see you have your father's temper," the bishop in black said, as if that ought to be an insult. His accent was decidedly French.

A second councilor, the one most often seen at the king's other shoulder, and never far away from the bishop in black, was a shorter, fairer man, with a heavy chain of office draped over his shoulders and unbowed by the weight of it.

He looked the bishop up and down and said, "Our fierce young Englishmen must seem so troublesome to you, my lord bishop."

The bishop offered a thin, indulgent smile. "Only when they overdrink, as Englishmen are wont."

This was an argument that had nothing to with John, who was only a little baffled and thinking he was drawing too much of the wrong kind of attention. "My lords," he said. "I really don't have my father's temper, but I do have his talent for talking too much and laughing when I shouldn't." To the king he said, "Your Grace, I am most sorry for disturbing your tournament."

"We cannot blame you for defending your sister, Lord John," the boy said. John bowed, grateful for his understanding. Because yes, he would defend Mary, come what may. He just didn't necessarily want Mary to know about it. Just now, Mary was so focused on the task at hand, she never noticed the altercation.

John tried to think of some joke to lighten the mood, but his wit failed him. They turned back to watch the final round of shooting. Arrows sang, thumped into straw bales. Archers shaded their eyes to see targets. The master archer himself had to measure, to see who had scored best, and at last proclaimed Mary of Locksley the winner.

~

Mary only partly expected the Sheriff of Nottingham or someone like him to spring out from behind the viewing stands and declare that this had all been a trap and that she would now be arrested for something or other. Except these days, the Sheriff of Nottingham was a conscientious middle-aged man who was cordial to the Locksleys. Lady Marian and his wife often exchanged herbal concoctions.

The master archer beamed at her, her rivals politely expressed their admiration, which she returned. All in all, Mary was a bit at a loss. Her shoulder ached. She rolled it back, wincing.

"Well done, Mary," John said, clapping her on the other shoulder. "You didn't even let Ranulf get to you."

"He was rude," she muttered.

"Never mind him."

She studied the crowd, but Ranulf FitzHugh had disappeared, which was just as well. Then she smiled suddenly.

"What?" John asked.

"I've stopped trying to look for William de Ros. So, this did some good after all."

"I'm not sure he even exists."

"That's what I think! Mother assured me he does—"

Eleanor came pushing through the crowd, head down and determined, until she reached Mary and grabbed her arm, beaming. Then the king arrived among them and was as happy as any of them had seen him. A flurry of bows rippled out from him like a wave.

"That was marvelous!" he exclaimed, face alight, grinning. "My lady, your prize!" Very proudly, he handed over the gold ring.

"Thank you, Your Grace," Mary said, bowing deeply, honored and blushing in spite of herself. The ring only fit on her thumb, so she put it there, and the king seemed so very pleased.

"Your father must be proud of you. Is he here?"

Mary said, "I'm afraid he had business elsewhere, but yes, I believe he's proud of us."

"Lady Eleanor, you weren't with your brother and sister among the archers," the king said. "Do you shoot as well?"

She shook her head shyly and hid behind Mary's shoulder.

"I beg your pardon, sire," Mary said quickly, before the king could take offense. "Our sister doesn't speak. She has no voice."

He raised a brow, interested. Perhaps skeptical. Mary had a sinking feeling then, that if this boy mocked Eleanor or caused her any hurt at all, she would knock him to the ground. John had stepped forward, probably with the same thought. They would both knock the boy down, and then they would all hang, so she desperately hoped Henry did nothing of the kind.

"Why not?" he asked simply.

Mary hesitated a moment, then nudged their sister forward, out of her shelter. "Ask her."

"Lady Eleanor, why don't you speak?"

The girl took a moment to gather herself, looking for all the world like someone deciding on what words to use. Then, she clenched her fists at her throat, squeezed her eyes tight, and it perfectly conveyed the idea of pain and choking. Of speech locked tightly away, never to escape. She flicked her fingers away, then settled her hands at her sides. Her voice scattered, dead. She pursed her lips and bowed her head.

"Our sympathies to you," he said.

Her expression turned suddenly bright, blushing. This meaning too was somehow clear: she did not mind, it was just the way things were. One could not help but smile with her.

"She does speak, in her own way," John said. "She shoots as well. But she doesn't much like crowds."

"Indeed." Henry gazed out over the pitch again with wonder and frank longing. "We should have more contests like this. I wish I could shoot so well. *Half* so well." He was definitely the boy now, not the king.

John said, "It's mostly a matter of practice——"

"It's more than that, you said so yourself," Henry replied. "Though it's true, I get very little chance to practice. It's unseemly." He frowned. That was someone else's word for it, Mary wagered, eyeing the serious old men behind him. "I've never even climbed a tree," the king sighed.

"Really?" John said, astonished, and then thoughtful.

The somber bishop, who was never far from the king—and who no doubt thought shooting arrows and climbing trees was unseemly—came forward, glancing at the Locksley children with a look of distaste.

"Your Grace, we must away, if you please. There are important matters to attend to." His accent marked him as French—from the continent. He gestured out of the pavilion.

"Well, then," King Henry said. "We hope to see you all again soon."

They bowed once again—it felt excessive, but then, one would rather bow too much than too little. But for just a moment there, he hadn't seemed like the king.

"Imagine," John said, looking after them. "By right the most powerful man in England, and he's called away to lessons. And never climbed a tree."

"Let's go back to camp," Mary said, putting her arm around Eleanor's shoulders. "I've had enough."

Mary had been thinking of how she was supposed to know if she liked William de Ros, when—if—she finally met him. Father had said she would not have to marry him if she didn't like him. But how would she know, at one meeting? He could be on his best behavior for one meeting, and then turn horrible after they were married, once he had her and she would have to spend the rest of her life with him. Or she could always run away to Sherwood . . .

She had begun to have some idea of how she might tell if she liked a man or not. Ranulf FitzHugh at the tournament—she would not marry him if he were the last man in the world. Many of the men at the tournament, ones who looked her up and down while wearing a scowl—she disliked them all. Many men were nice enough at the start; they had pretty manners and would bow and smile fondly at women—and then ignore them, as if they didn't merit further attention. So, while they were not cruel, they were not . . . likable. She began to watch how men treated their servants and animals. Anyone weaker than they. Did they look their servants in the eye, speak kindly, or at least not cruelly? Did they pet their horses' necks or take a moment to scratch their hounds' ears? Did their animals cringe from them or seek out contact? She would contrive to watch William de Ros with a pack of hounds. Before she would let him add her to his kennel, ha.

Some men were handsome, and she wanted to meet these men and hoped they were likable. She would see some young man, smiling as he rode by on a beautifully turned-out horse, or simply glancing over his shoulder in a certain way, and wish very much that *that* one was William de Ros . . . She determined that maybe she shouldn't be thinking about men quite so much.

She just wanted to *know*.

Eleanor ran ahead. John was quiet, which made Mary suspicious.

"What are you thinking?" she asked finally.

After a thoughtful pause he said, "Best you don't know."

"John—"

He strode ahead, almost running like Eleanor, so he would not have to answer.

At the Locksley encampment, Mother and her maid Beatrice sat by the fire with a basket of sewing. The baron was looking over some piece of leather tack for the horses with Will Scarlet.

Eleanor had already taken up a seat by Marian, who brightened when the others arrived. "How was it?"

"Mary won," John said, and they responded with a generally embarrassing hurrah.

"Well done!" Robin said.

"I didn't split it but I got close." She drew the gouged arrow from her quiver and tossed it to him.

Robin caught it and traced the wound in the shaft. "One of these days, you'll split one."

"Seems a waste of a good arrow to me," she said, hanging up her gear on the rack. She sat by the fire and accepted a cup of wine from Beatrice.

"Always the practical one," he said, laughing. "And what do you make of our young king?"

She hesitated. She had a lot of thoughts about the king and wasn't sure which was the most important. "He was kind to Eleanor," she said finally.

Robin was taken aback. "Well, that is something."

"You were right," John said. "He's lonely. His advisors watch him closely."

"Who is the tall one in black? The French-born bishop who never lets the king out of his sight?" Mary asked.

"That is Peter des Roches, the Bishop of Winchester. No one outside of the court trusts him, but to his credit, I think he cares about the boy."

"And the other one?" John asked. "The fair one with the big chain of office?"

"Hubert de Burgh, Chief Justiciar of England, appointed by the late King. He was King John's man through and through." Robin didn't need to elaborate—the English barons might see de Burgh as one of their own, unlike des Roches, but Robin himself would never trust him. No wonder Robin of Locksley wanted to stay out of it all. The baron turned pensive. "Since William Marshal died, those two will be after each other for power. Marshal kept them in check—no one could argue with him. But now . . ." He shook his head.

"How do you deal with men like that?" John asked. "Henry is king but they hold the power, that much is clear."

"Mostly, you stay out of their way," Robin said.

"You'll notice your father rarely follows his own advice." Marian innocently stitched at a sleeve.

"They always meddle with me, not the other way around," Robin protested.

"Yes, love." She smiled sweetly.

"That doesn't help," John said. "I can try to curry favor with Henry all I like, until they shut the door. They don't seem very enamored of the name of Locksley." John narrowed his gaze accusingly at Robin.

Marian said, "I think what your father is saying is don't *try* to curry favor. Rather, be honest and honorable. Just be yourself."

"Yes, that is exactly what I'm saying. Listen to your mother. She's much better at these things than I am." The pair traded one of those adoring looks that always made the minstrels swoon.

Mary looked on, astonished. *Just be himself?* They had no idea what they'd just unleashed, did they?

~

Sneaking past Will Scarlet might be nearly impossible. In fact, if John could do that much, the rest of the plan would seem easy.

Will set a couple of his assistants to keep watch through the night—he did not call them guards, but that was what they were. The guards would be looking for people coming into camp, not out of camp, so that was something. Will himself would walk a circuit once more before he retired. If John waited until after that hour, it would be too late for what he intended. So, he had to sneak out before, even though it meant avoiding the watch.

After dark, the fire in the camp's forecourt blazed, and

Robin presided over a small gathering of old friends. Not the barons and would-be allies, the men of politics who wanted to strategize about where they stood with the new king and old charters and the like. That had happened earlier. This was different—these were the old foresters and former outlaws who had been with him in Sherwood a quarter-century before. John longed to sit among them and listen to stories, hoping for the ones he hadn't heard before, the more harrowing tales and near misses and hardships that didn't get sung about. There were two versions of what had happened, and they didn't talk about the true version among outsiders. For all that he was Robin's son, John would always be an outsider because he had not been there.

However much he wanted to, John didn't stay, but pretended to go to bed and then crept to the back of the camp while Robin and Will Scarlet and Dav and the others had their attention on the fire and their cups of ale. Their tents blocked the light; he was able to stay in shadow and move slowly and quietly so as not to draw attention. His sisters were in their tent, and John didn't want his silhouette splashing across the canvas. Mary would stop him. Eleanor would want to go with him.

Carefully then, he put space between himself and the camp. He reached the copse of trees, waited to see if any alarm was raised. Then he jogged out to the path that led to the palace.

The place was busy, even at this hour, with messengers and attendants coming and going, horses riding in and out. And yes, guards. But John was dressed well and looked like he belonged. He had merely to act like it, too, and to have a story ready if anyone stopped him and asked what he was doing here.

He hadn't quite thought of a believable story yet. He could say he was some man's squire, but which man? If he claimed to be a messenger, from whom was the message? And to whom, and what about? He would be asked all these things, and no excuse he thought of seemed reasonable.

Boldly, he walked past two sword-carrying guards at the gate in the palace's outer courtyard. No one stopped him. Next, he made it through the stable yard, which was crowded enough John merely had to act like one of the stable hands, stewards, and young lords fussing over their hounds and horses.

Then he was inside, striding through a passageway that opened to a hall full of rowdy feasting. Losing himself here would be easy, though clearly these folk had far more rank and wealth than he. Dukes and earls, royal attendants, cousins of the king and all their hangers-on. Hooded falcons huddled on perches; hounds scrabbled for bones in the corners. He took a place by the stone wall and had a look around. If King Henry was here, he might be allowed to approach and even speak his plan to him outright. The high table stood at the back of the hall, but it was empty except for a handful of men clustered at one end, talking. One of them was the Bishop of Winchester, des Roches. Which meant that the king was currently unsupervised, perhaps. If John could just get to him . . .

The further into this rarefied realm he went, the less believable any lie he could tell to explain himself would be. He was already an intruder. He could almost hear Mary hissing at him, *You will hang for this.*

He was certain he wouldn't. For today at least, because of the tournament, he had the king's favor.

Moving out of the hall, he found a smaller courtyard with several doorways leading to different sets of chambers. He studied each of them, then approached the one that had armed guards standing by. Acting like he belonged here was harder than it had been when he was surrounded by other people and could use the noise and activity as a cover. Here, he walked down the corridor alone. He passed a serving woman with a tray. She took a quick glance at him; he ignored her because that was what would be expected. The guards marked his approach.

John stopped before them and announced himself. "I

am Lord John of Locksley. His Grace the king has summoned me." His tone was completely serious and offered no room for argument. Or rather, if they wanted to argue, they would have to do so with the king.

They might have done well to ask if King Henry had really summoned him, and why. But astonishingly, they didn't question him at all. One of the guards nodded, went through the door behind him, and returned just a few moments later.

"His Grace is waiting for you, my lord," he said, and stepped aside to gesture John through.

Praise be to God, this might actually work. Or he would hang for it. Trying to strike a balance between confidence and caution, he entered King Henry's chamber.

The room was small but richly furnished and warm, with a blazing hearth and many candles, tapestries on the wall and seats with cushions. The windows were high and narrow, and another door likely led to the bedchamber. Henry sat in this front room, next to a table which held a platter with a mostly eaten meal and a jug of wine. He was dressed simply, compared to how he'd been over the last several days. A wool tunic with fine trim over a linen shift, a fur-lined coat. No crown or circlet on his head. A serving boy was there tending the fire, and Henry said to him, "You may go."

The boy bowed and fled out the door John had just

entered. The king studied him, and John prepared to apologize profusely.

"Lord John," Henry said evenly.

"Your Grace," he said, bowing as formally and graciously as he knew how. Which he feared was not very. The king remained silent. "Sire—you might need to have a word with your guards. That was a lot easier than it should have been."

"*What* was a lot easier?"

"Um. Getting in here. I only wanted to see if I could, just to have a word with you. I must have looked *really* harmless, which is sort of discouraging if I think about it—"

"Lord John, why are you here?" The boy sounded ancient and careworn. John ought to apologize and leave. For all he knew, the king had given the guard instructions to return with half the army and all the knights and bishops besides . . .

Instead, John smiled slyly and said, "Mischief."

Henry's frown remained, but only for a moment. Then his eyes lit. "Oh? What sort of mischief?"

"There is a very fine orchard behind the cloister gardens. The trees there may not be the best for climbing. But they are climbable."

Henry stared. "It's the middle of the night."

"Even better."

Gaze narrowed, he sat back, obviously thinking. "So, you came here, entered my chamber under false pretenses, and are proposing we sneak out without guards or attendants or anything, just so we can climb trees in the orchard in the middle of the night?"

"Yes, exactly." The worst would have been if Henry had been baffled and totally unwilling, and John would have had to creep away in shame.

"I'm not allowed to go out without at least a guard. Or at all, after dark."

"If I find us a way to sneak out of here, can you promise me I won't hang for it if we're caught?"

"If you promise me you weren't sent by the King of France to kidnap me for ransom."

"My liege, no, of course not—Wait, have the French actually tried that?"

"There have been spies," he said darkly.

John sympathized deeply. No wonder Henry was so serious. "I promise you I'm not a spy. I only thought it was awful that you'd never climbed a tree."

Henry stood and smoothed out his tunic in a practiced gesture. "Well then, Lord John. I would like to climb a tree."

"Very good, sire." He made a quick circuit of the chamber. The windows here were too high and narrow. The next room, which was even smaller, didn't have windows at all, only a brazier and a sleeping box with mussed-up blankets. But there was a second door, small and cup-board-like. An escape route.

Henry watched him studying the room's layout. "Perhaps we could summon the serving boy, and we could trade clothes and I walk out—"

"What sort of punishment would he receive, if he were discovered?" John asked.

Henry said, "Whipped and turned out."

"Then no, we must risk only ourselves," John said. "Where does this door go?"

"To the next hall."

It was the sort of door to let a mistress come and go unseen, but John didn't mention that. "You ever try sneaking out?"

"Only to go to chapel, and only when there aren't so many people around."

How somber a boy did one have to be to sneak out to go to chapel? That was a question for another time. Carefully, John tried the door, hoping it was not secured from the outside. But that would make it a terrible bolt-hole. It swung inward, and he eased it open an inch or two. Darkness lay outside—because the door was hidden behind a tapestry. Which meant perhaps it was not being watched.

They needed to get outside as quickly as possible, preferably in a way that no one would see them. How far did the boy's authority really go? Couldn't he simply order anyone he saw to let them go? And they would report back to de Burgh or des Roches. Somehow, getting by on the orders of the king felt like cheating. How much more fun to get away without anyone seeing them at all?

"Give me a minute, sire. Wait here, I will return."

Around the near corner, the guards stood watch at the main door. John avoided them, turning the other way. He moved quickly, with purpose, listening closely for voices. At the next corner, an archway exited to a walk that led to the abbey grounds.

He returned to the tapestry, where Henry was waiting, eagerly gripping the edge of the door. Now John had only to tell the King of England what to do. No, not the king. A co-conspirator.

He spoke softly. "Your Grace, we must move quickly but without rushing. We walk with purpose, so no one who sees us will think of stopping us."

"But we do have a purpose."

"Yes, but we want to avoid looking guilty about it. We want to look like we're *not* sneaking."

"Ah."

"We walk down the center of the corridor, just two young lords out for a stroll. Do you have a cap? And leave the cloak behind, it'll only get in the way."

Grinning now, Henry did all this, put on a dark nondescript cap and left the cloak on the bed. Oh, God, John really was going to hang for this. He was corrupting the king. He quickly put the thought aside and moved on.

As it happened, Henry was good at following instructions. John thought back to the coronation, the boy sitting so properly, speaking so properly, never wavering through the precise drudgery of the ritual. Suddenly, John wondered if he was doing the king a great service, teaching him to rebel. Just a little.

More quickly than John expected, they were outside. The night was cool and damp, the sky heavy but without rain. The sounds of revelry from the front of the palace drifted over, the light of torches turning the hazy air orange. But on this side, all was dark and peaceful. The abbey church loomed, a few faint lights shining through glass windows. Ahead, gardens and the abbey's stone walls. Beyond, orchards and pastures.

The young king paused a moment, looking up and around. He stretched his arms, shuddered like a horse shaking off a harness.

"This way, sire," John said, and nodded to a packed-dirt path leading into the darkness. Then they ran.

The nighttime orchard was nothing like Sherwood. The pale trees were lined up in neat rows; the ground beneath them was well groomed. The branches were full of new spring leaves and budding flowers. The foliage was thin enough, hiding would be more difficult. No mind; they wouldn't be here long. Just an hour or so, until the king grew cold and had his fill of this small adventure.

"The trick is to find a low branch, but not too low. One you can reach by jumping and is strong enough to take your weight." He found a likely tree, one with lots of spreading branches that would be easy enough to climb. John jumped up to it, a foot on the trunk, a hand on one branch, using momentum to propel himself upward. He paused, standing on a branch, holding the one above it.

The king looked back up at him, face screwed up, clearly daunted.

"Just try," John said.

"You've been doing this your whole life. You must have been born in a tree."

John laughed. "My mother would not have put up with that."

Henry pushed up his sleeves, which promptly slipped back down, and reached for the first branch. He moved slowly, methodically, struggled to pull himself up, but then got an arm over, then swung a leg, and suddenly he was straddling the branch, gazing around in amazement.

John climbed to the next branch up to give him more room. Henry stood—carefully, keeping a hand on the trunk—and followed John up. They were a dozen feet off the ground now, and through the tree's branches had a sweeping view of the church and village, and the wide sparkling stretch of the Thames beyond.

"You'll have to come to Sherwood and see the old oaks," John said. "You could build a whole village in the trees there."

"The stories make more sense now," Henry said. "If the foresters don't look up, they'd never see you here. Standing still, dressed in green, you'd look like just another branch."

"I'll tell you a secret: they hardly ever look up. It's magical."

"Did your father teach you to climb trees?"

John furrowed his brow. He couldn't remember *not* climbing trees. "I don't really remember. He mostly just set us loose. I'd follow Mary around—she loves the forest. It drove me mad when she went off to the woods and left me behind."

"I didn't learn a single thing from my father except how to make everyone furious."

Cautiously, John said, "You didn't know him well."

"I can't remember the last time I saw him before he died. He just ... he was never there. I do remember once he came to look me over and said, 'He's very small, isn't he?' And I think it must have been Lord Peter who said, 'He is a child, Your Grace.' And my father said, 'Show him to us again when he's bigger.' Then he

died before I could get any bigger. Your father probably knew him better than I ever did." Henry looked up
at him, his brow furrowed. "What does Lord Robin say
about my father?"

"I had better not tell you what Lord Robin says about
your father."

"Nobody liked him," Henry said sullenly. "Even those
who served him only did so to win power for themselves.
They only serve me for the same reason."

John did not think this was true. Not when the boy
was so earnest and trying so hard to be likable. One must
want to help him. "Your Grace, I think they serve you because that is what is best for England. If they are good
men, that is."

Henry's expression remained screwed up and worried.

The sound of voices reached them, low and urgent.
Henry flinched, searching, and John put a hand on his
shoulder.

"Stay very, very still, sire," he whispered. Both of them
pressed close to the tree's trunk and froze.

He spotted the men soon enough, three of them in
heavy cloaks coming through the orchard, all hunched
together. He couldn't see much else, such as if they went
armed or who they might be.

" . . . by the water," one of them said. "It must look as if
he drowned."

They seemed to be making for the river's edge, past the cloister gardens.

"What of the letter? Have you put it with him?"

"In a moment—damn you, he's slipping!"

Cursing at each other, they stumbled to a stop very near the tree where the boys watched. Henry grabbed John's sleeve, his eyes round and his face gone pale. John had seen it.

The three cloaked men were carrying a body.

~

Mary had retired to the ladies' tent for the evening when Eleanor rushed in, grabbed her arm in a panic, and pointed out.

"It's John, isn't it?" Mary asked. "He's gone to do something stupid." The youngest Locksley nodded, and Mary muttered, "I knew it. Well, I suppose we'll have to go after him."

Voices filled the camp's front court, speaking low and punctuated by occasional laughter. What good would it do to announce to their parents that John had run off? It would create a stir that would embarrass them and perhaps get her brother in more trouble than he was already in—however much he might deserve it. Besides, she thought she knew exactly where John had gone. He'd never get away with what he had planned, if he was attempting what she feared.

"Out the back, yes?" Mary asked. Eleanor went to the front flap, glanced out to have a look, and nodded.

Mary looked around a moment. She was still in her kirtle but had pulled off her veil for the evening, leaving her dark hair braided down her back. She ought to cover her head if she was going out, but the stark white linen would only draw attention at night. Eleanor had abandoned hers much earlier in the day.

Besides, no one would see them, not if they were careful.

Pulling out a stake, she released one of the tent's back flaps. The girls crept out, shut the flap behind them. No lanterns or torches lit this side of camp. Mary paused for her sight to adjust to the dark.

"Anything the matter, my ladies?"

Flinching, Mary touched her chest, near her suddenly pounding heart. Eleanor's hands clutched her skirt. There stood Will Scarlet, arms crossed, standing at the next tent as if he had just paused to admire the stars in the sky.

Mary couldn't come up with a reasonable lie, and Eleanor certainly wasn't going to provide an explanation.

"John's run off to do something foolish. We're going to bring him back."

Will straightened, concerned. "I didn't see him leave. Are you sure?"

"Check his bed," Mary said, scowling.

"Should I be worried?"

"Oh, probably."

"But you know where he's gone?"

She hesitated. "I think so."

A pause, as he waited for her to tell him. He blew out a frustrated breath. "All right, don't tell me. I trust you to be sensible. You'll find him and bring him straight back, yes? Many strange folk are about. You shouldn't be out at all."

"Yes, I know. We'll be back as quick as we can."

"This isn't like Sherwood. You don't know the ground here. There's no Little John to look after you."

"I suppose you'll go to Mother and Father with this?"

"I'll tell them . . . *if* you don't come straight back."

"Thank you, Will." No reason to draw them into it and make a fuss. Will touched his cap and vanished back to the shadows like a wraith.

Mary held Eleanor's hand and set off.

Out of sight of camp, Eleanor took off running. Mary almost shouted after her from pure habit but stopped herself. Catching up with her sister, she was able to steer her away from the main track that led from the encampments to the village. Keeping to copses and hedgerows, they skirted around, heading for the palace. Took longer, but it wouldn't do to be seen. Sweat from nerves and exercise chilled in the night air, and Mary shivered. Her brother was an idiot. He wouldn't get past the main courtyard of the palace, much less to the king's chambers. At least she didn't think he would.

Then again, he might.

She touched Eleanor's shoulder. "Do you suppose there are any trees near the palace?"

Eleanor pointed past the garden and a set of pastures, to an apple orchard near the edge of the abbey grounds. He could have found so many better ways to show the king how to climb trees. Invite him to a hunt at Sherwood, ask the guards to politely stand watch and perhaps catch the boy if he slipped and fell. But she suspected half the fun for John was in the sneaking out.

He would *hang* for this . . .

Traveling along the pasture to the first of the trees, Mary paused, scowling, but Eleanor seemed eager. She wasn't angry John had sneaked off, Mary realized; she was angry John had left her behind.

They heard voices. Eleanor clasped Mary's arm and pointed; Mary pulled her close to the tree and held her still.

They had been looking for two boys. Instead, a trio of cloaked men stumbled down the middle of the orchard. Drunken revelers got lost on their way back to their camps, maybe. However, at the end of the row of trees, one of them stumbled, the group lurched to a halt, cursing.

And they dropped the body they'd been carrying.

Mary swallowed back a gasp and held her sister close. They must hide, whatever was happening here, they could not draw attention to themselves, they must—

A young man leapt out of the nearby tree, shouting, landing on the closest of the men. This was John, of course.

One of the men immediately ran off, perhaps thinking he was being charged by a bear or a demon or something more dangerous than a sixteen-year-old boy. The man John had landed on cried and lashed out while John pummeled him. The third lunged toward John. This one had a dagger in hand.

Mary had nothing, no weapons, no bow and arrow. Wildly, she looked around and found a rake and a bucket propped up against the next tree over, left by some gardener. She grabbed them both and ran, Eleanor on her heels.

Screaming, brandishing the rake overhead, she hoped to make herself sound like an army as she charged straight for the fight and swung the rake hard at the knifeman's head. He let out a rash of curses, ducked, stumbled back. She kept going, bringing the rake up and over and throwing the bucket at him. John kicked at the other one as he clambered to his feet to run after his comrade. Abandoned, even the knifeman left off and chased after his fellows. All were crying out the most blasphemous curses, fleeing across the orchard and past the shelter of a hedgerow. Mary leaned on the rake and watched.

John had the nerve to laugh. "I think we surprised them."

Eleanor knelt beside the body the men had left behind, touching his neck, then holding her palm over his mouth. She looked up at Mary with urgency, wearing a thin smile that seemed hopeful. Mary joined her, touched the vein at the body's neck—

"He's not dead," she said.

He was a young man with brown hair neatly trimmed above his ears, his face clean-shaven. He wore a neat, dark tunic and coat.

John joined them, to see for himself. "Perhaps he's drunk?"

"There's no smell of ale on him."

Eleanor ran fingers over the man's head, then held up her hand to show the others: there was blood.

"That was *wonderful!*" King Henry exclaimed. Awkwardly but with great enthusiasm, he clung to a branch and lowered himself from the tree, dropping the last few feet. "You fought off those men with nothing but your hands and a rake!"

"They didn't do very much fighting," John said. "They weren't fighters."

Mary hurriedly stood, flushing till her cheeks burned. This was the king, and here they were out in the middle of the night with would-be murderers . . . She curtseyed. "Your Grace, please excuse my brother's awful behavior and recklessness—"

"Be easy, Lady Mary. We're having an adventure! And we have saved this man's life, I think."

He was right. "But what were those men doing with him?"

"Is there a letter?" John asked. "One of them said something about a letter." Eleanor patted down the man's coat, looked in the pouch at his belt, then shook her head.

"I know this man," Henry said, crouching to look more closely at his face. "He's one of Lord Peter's clerks."

"Peter des Roches?" Mary exclaimed.

John added, "They talked of drowning him."

Eleanor had started shaking his shoulder and patting his cheeks.

"Eleanor, that may not be such—"

The young man groaned and batted clumsily at his

head. Eleanor took his hands and folded them to his chest. Mary knelt to touch his face.

"Sir? Sir, can you hear me? Can you tell me your name?"

"Ah . . . Walter? Where . . ."

"You've been attacked," she said. "What do you remember?"

"Something . . . hit me from behind. I don't know what. It all went dark." The man looked around, and his gaze rested on Henry. "Oh God, my liege!" He tried to sit up and immediately rolled to his side and moaned worryingly.

Voices came through the orchard again, and the figures of men stalked toward them through the trees. Four of them this time, moving with determination. One of them had a lantern, a speck of light dangling at his side. Another had a sword. They might have fetched a guard. A troop prepared for a hunt.

"We have to get out of here," John murmured.

"Walter, you've got to get up," Mary said, and drew one of his arms over her shoulder. John got the other. Eleanor picked up the rake. "Your Grace—"

"Henry," he said. "Call me Henry."

That seemed a vast gulf to cross, an enormous breach of manners, but she nodded. "Henry. We can get help at the abbey, I think."

"The way is blocked," John said. The approaching men were between them and the abbey grounds beyond the orchard. "We'll have to go around."

"To the palace, then?" Mary asked.

"Just away!"

The hedgerow that bordered the orchard offered some shelter. Sticking close to it, they crept as fast as they could, hauling the still-vague Walter. The rake Eleanor carried was taller than she was, making her seem like some fairy soldier guarding the king.

Henry kept looking behind. "There's more of them. I see six now. Two with swords."

"Good God, who are they?"

"They're dressed like clerks. Except the two guards, that is. I do not know them."

They came to a gap in the hedgerow and ducked through. The tangle of vegetation was nothing like the oaks of Sherwood, which Mary missed terribly just now.

Across the field, the first of the encampments huddled, pale tents showing bright even without moonlight on them. "We'll find help among the camps," Mary said.

"Not all those camps are friendly," John put in.

Henry started eagerly, "Your father's camp—"

Mary shook her head. "On the other side of the field and well apart. He doesn't much like being too close to anyone."

John sighed. "Surely we can find someone close by. We have the king with us, for God's sake!"

"I do not like to say it," Mary said, "but a good number of these barons are still rebels at heart and might like to have his Grace—Henry—land in their laps, to do with him as they please."

"God, that's devious," John said, and she could not tell if his tone was aghast or admiring.

"I am not afraid of anyone," Henry declared. But he did not deny that someone might try to hold him hostage, sell him to the French, or worse.

Eleanor tugged on Mary's sleeve; the men were closing on them.

John eased Walter off his shoulder. "Eleanor, give me that," he said, taking the rake from her. "I'll lead them away while the rest of you get help."

"Absolutely not! You'll be killed!" Mary said.

"I won't. Wait and see." He grinned, bowed to the king, and trotted off.

"John!"

King Henry looked after him wistfully, and Mary wondered how she would stop him from following. Or perhaps they could simply show Henry and use him as a shield to get back to the abbey—

"Will he be all right?" Henry asked worriedly.

"He has been so far," Mary conceded.

"Your Grace, *I* will go to the abbey and get help," Walter said carefully, still wobbling.

"You're not well, sir," Mary said.

John trotted along the hedgerow, rake over his shoulder, collecting rocks as he went. He made a spectacle of himself, throwing rocks at their pursuers until they shouted, pointed, and gave chase. Then he ducked through to the other side of the hedge and out of sight.

That was it, their chance to move unseen. "Come on, to the end of the field, then we can turn back to the abbey. Eleanor—"

But Eleanor was gone.

～

Leading bad men on a merry chase was not as easy in an open field as it was in Sherwood. Why were there no forests around Westminster? Instead, nothing but miles and miles of pastures and fields full of grains and turnips. If John could get these fellows turned around so that they didn't know where they were, he'd consider the job done. Alas, the great spires of the abbey church rose up like a beacon to mark their place. No one could ever get lost around here, not really. And John did not know this land, where the streams and glens were, which were the best places to hide, and where to set traps. Fortunately, these were town and court men, like as not to trip over clods of dirt in the countryside. Still, their daggers and swords would run him through well enough if they caught up to him. The lantern one of them carried drew ever closer.

He squeezed through the branches of the hedgerow and waited.

Six men, as Henry had said. Were they following some lord's orders, or was this a petty disagreement against poor Walter? And what of the letter they spoke of? It didn't matter. John had only to keep them busy while Mary got the others away.

"Where'd he go?" one of the men asked.

"Who is it?"

"I didn't recognize him."

"Who would be out here at this time of night? No one knows we're here—"

"Obviously, someone does! There are spies everywhere!"

"We will simply have to tell de Burgh we failed . . ."

Hubert de Burgh? Why would he send men after des Roches' clerk? Was Walter a spy or turncoat? Then why not simply accuse him outright and have him arrested? This was some conspiracy. Kill des Roches' clerk, but make it look like he was murdered or had some mishap on the road, with a letter planted on him . . . This was some conspiracy. And now there was a witness to it, whom they could not very well let go. Well, this was a nice puzzle, wasn't it?

"Maybe he didn't see anything—"

"They've taken that clerk away. They saw everything!"

John tumbled out of the hedgerow and ran.

"There he is!"

The crowd of de Burgh's men chased him, which was what he wanted. If only he knew what to do next. He had a rake, a knife at his belt, and his own two legs. At least he was faster than them. He raced for the nearby river, away from the abbey. They charged after him. All of them, which meant none were chasing after Mary and the others.

Thank God they didn't have arrows. However, they could pick up rocks just as easily as he could. One of them threw one, which hit John's leg and skittered ahead. The hit stung; he kept running.

If he could reach the river, he might jump in and swim for the other side. He suspected these men wouldn't be eager to get wet and would let him go. But he feared now he wouldn't reach the river in time. More rocks flew at him.

One struck his shoulder, and he stumbled. Lost some ground. The men fanned out, surrounding him. Hounds, bringing a fox to bay. John still had the rake; he could still fight, so he turned and held the rake like a quarterstaff, just like Little John had taught him.

Two of them had swords. The rest had knives, and half of them had rocks in their hands. Maybe he could talk his way out of this. "What's this letter you spoke of? Something incriminating to the Bishop of Winchester, I gather. You leave it to be found with his dead clerk—"

"You see?" one of them hissed at the others. "You talked so much and he's heard everything—"

"Quiet!" another answered.

John marked all their faces. Several clerks like Walter, a pair of common soldiers. Some clean-shaven, some with trimmed beards. But yes, he could recognize them again if he needed to. Which meant they'd be very eager to kill him now. He laughed, tried to think of something clever to say—his father would say something clever just now. But he couldn't think of what so had to make do with the laughter.

"Kill him, dump his body in the river."

"This is a bad idea, Philip."

The other, presumably Philip, hissed at him to shut up.

"I know this boy," yet another of them said. "He's Robin of Locksley's son."

"Robin of Locksley! Why, we can hold him for ransom!"

"Better men than you have tried that," John said. "They're dead now."

"Shut up, boy. You've doomed yourself."

"I don't think so," he countered. He wished he could come up with something clever and cutting, but he just kept thinking, *Wait until my father hears of this,* and he refused to say that out loud.

They crept forward. He danced backward—he might still be able to throw himself in the river to escape—and swung the rake to keep a space around himself. He could only keep this up for so long. The minute they decided to all charge at once, he was done for.

But none of them wanted to be the first one to be struck. One of them would have to let himself be struck, to give the others the opening they needed. These men were not fighters and had no sense of tactics. Even the ones with the swords seemed uncertain.

Finally, the pair with swords lunged at him at the same time. John feinted with the rake, smacked one then the other on the wrists, moving faster than he ever had in his life. Swung the rake again; stumbled when he tried to back out.

An arrow struck the ground between two of the attackers, hitting with a sudden *thunk.* The line of cloaked men scattered. Another arrow struck, and another. The men turned to look for this new attack, but in the dark they could see nothing. The other side of the field was all shadow.

Then the lantern was struck, the glass bursting, the candle going out. Its bearer dropped it, jumped away, screamed.

"What is it!" one of the men cried.

"We are discovered, run!" said another.

They fled in all directions, into the dark and the hedgerows where they must have thought they could find shelter. John was forgotten, crouching with the rake behind a fence of arrows. None of them had gotten too close, as if the archer hadn't meant to hit anybody, merely frighten them.

John noticed: they weren't Locksley arrows with their plain gray feathers. He pulled one out of the ground, studied it. Brown fletching, unremarkable. If it wasn't a Locksley who'd fired the shot, then who?

Out of habit, he collected all the arrows. Then he ran to where the archer must have stood.

~

"John went out, and Mary and Eleanor followed?" Robin said. He was pacing, while Will Scarlet stood off to the side, gaze downcast and chagrined. Will said they had been gone for more than an hour, after promising to be back quickly, which meant that either they had found additional mischief or they were in trouble.

Marian refused to be angry, and definitely refused to be frightened. She sat by the fire, working with spindle and wool, which was easier in the dark than embroidery or mending, to try to calm herself. She hated to think what sort of mischief they might encounter with so many strangers around. They were good children, really. Except they were very nearly no longer children at all. Mary was full grown. Marian just didn't like to admit it.

"I didn't expect John to be able to sneak out. I'm sorry—"

"Don't apologize—I'm impressed he got past you," Robin said. "And the girls? You just let them go?"

"Mary didn't try to lie, and she insisted they'd be back soon."

Frowning, Robin looked out toward the torch and lantern lights of Westminster, setting the nighttime mist aglow. "She must have known where John was going."

"She wouldn't say."

"Those conniving little kits, what have they got up to?"

"Rob, I'm sure they're fine, they're just out exploring—"

"Should we go after them?" Robin was so rarely uncertain about anything. "There are a dozen men within an arrow's flight who would use them to hurt me."

"They wouldn't dare, not under the king's nose like this," Marian said, but was unconvinced.

"The king's got nothing to say about anything," Robin said. "He's no older than they are—*oh*." He sank onto a bench and ran tired hands through his hair.

Marian and Will exchanged a glance. "Robin?" she tested.

"I told him that he should be friends with the king. The boy took me at my word. What trouble has he gotten that poor child into?"

She needed a few moments to catch up with him, and then was astonished. "You're saying he's gone off to . . . what? Drag the king into some boyish pranks?"

"And Mary guessed, so she went after him. Eleanor never likes to be left out of anything. And . . ." He shook his head, defeated. "They've been gone for *hours*!"

On the one hand, Marian was furious that the children would be so foolish to go out in a strange place at night. On the other, perhaps the young king might like a bit of harmless mischief. How much trouble could they really get into with that very well-guarded young man in tow?

"Well," Marian said calmly. "Perhaps they found an adventure."

"Marian, they were supposed to be nothing like me. They were supposed to be sensible and quiet and not at all prone to adventures."

"Hmm," she said, refusing to state any opinion about what Robin's children were meant to be like. If they were wild, she'd blame Sherwood Forest before she blamed Robin. Something about that place got into one's bones and made one rash.

Will went to the cask of ale to pour a couple of mugs and brought one to Robin. "Drink, my lord."

Robin tried, but just as he brought the mug to his lips, a fresh commotion traveled from the back of the camp. Dav of Doncaster and Grace had a young man between them, dragging him so he could not get his feet under him. Dav and Grace were two of Robin's company who'd left the forest to come with him to Locksley. Dav was lean, with a studious gaze, his dark beard now dusted with gray. Grace, a tall woman with a constant frown, dressed as a forester and kept her hair short. With her cap and leather jerkin, she was often mistaken for a man and she liked it that way. Middle-aged but no less hearty for it, they were unswervingly loyal.

Robin set down the mug. "God, this was supposed to be a peaceful night!" Marian set down her spinning to watch.

"What have you got here?" Will asked, on alert now, his hand tightening around the grip of his sword.

"Caught him sneaking around back," Dav said. The prisoner lunged, but Grace twisted his arm and dropped him to his knees at Robin's feet.

Robin of Locksley, lord of Sherwood, outlaw of legend, master of whatever realm he happened to find himself in, put hands on hips and looked down his nose at the man. Marian's breath still caught to see him like this, as it had the very first time she had set her gaze on him.

"Might I ask why you were sneaking into my camp, sir? You'd have been welcomed and offered wine if you'd come in the front."

The prisoner was high-born, the way he bucked and bristled at the handling these lowly foresters gave him. He might not even have noticed yet that Grace was a woman. "How dare you! I owe you no explanation—"

"Give me a name, then. Surely, you can do that much."

The man spat. So, high-born and foolish.

Marian rose from her bench and went to stand by her husband, her hands folded serenely. "This one is Berold FitzHugh's eldest son, I think. Ranulf FitzHugh, aren't you? Robin, you remember the FitzHughs?"

He thought for a moment, or pretended to, his gaze narrowed as he studied the irate young man. "Ah, yes. Had a habit of bribing old King John into granting him the lands of rebel barons, didn't he?"

"My father is loyal—"

"Lord Ranulf, why are you here?" Robin said, his tone growing iron.

The lad finally stopped fighting, as if he just now realized what he had gotten himself in to. "I . . . I . . . I wished to speak to your son. At the tournament . . . It's a matter of honor! It does not involve you, my lord."

"But this is my camp," Robin drawled. "A matter of honor, sneaking around the back? I don't think so."

Marian frowned. She did not like Ranulf, and did not like what any of this implied. "Dav, will you look at his hands? Do you think he uses a bow?"

Grace, a gleam in her eyes, held Ranulf while Dav yanked back his arms and had a look at his right hand, which would draw the string. He said, "Calluses, my lady. I think he does."

"Mary beat you at the tournament today, didn't she?" Marian said. "And you came here hoping to . . . what?"

"I told you, my purpose is with Lord John—"

"Then why not come in daylight?"

Ranulf glared. Beside her, Robin uncrossed his arms, squeezed his hands into fists. He was rarely so angry that he had no words or carried such darkness in his gaze.

Marian said softly, "My children can well look after themselves, as you'd have realized if you spent half a thought on the matter. So, what did you think would happen, coming here? Knowing who their father is?"

Ranulf was trapped. He had the look of a hound who had cornered a boar all by himself and then didn't know what to do with it. "Those . . . They're just stories. You aren't *him,* not really."

"No, of course not. That man lived a long time ago," Robin murmured. "I am much angrier right now than he ever was."

A log in the fire snapped, and sparks rose up. Marian shivered at the sound. Summer was nigh, but she was suddenly cold.

"My lord?" Will asked cautiously.

"Tie him," Robin said. "We will decide what to do with him before the night is out. And now I really need that mug of ale."

~

Eleanor was nowhere in sight. When the girl wanted to disappear, she was very good at it. But if she hadn't simply run off, if she had been taken, if there were murderers about and something happened—

"Where has she gone?" Mary said. "Did you see her?"

Henry was also looking around in a panic. "She's so quiet, I didn't hear a thing."

"Isn't that just like her. Eleanor is so quiet, poor Eleanor who can't speak, and she uses all that pity to get away with the worst kind of mischief!"

"But what if someone's caught her?"

If someone had caught her, she could not cry out for

help. Mary could shout her name all night long; her sister couldn't answer.

"Eleanor is very clever and isn't caught easily, but we must find her."

Stirring again, Walter said pleadingly, "Your Grace, what is happening?"

"Someone has tried to kill you."

"But *why*? My lady, let me go; I'm well enough now—" He pulled away from her grip and stumbled. Mary and Henry both caught him that time.

Deliver Walter to the abbey or look for Eleanor? Mary did not see how she could do both at once, and she dared not leave the king alone. No wonder Robin Hood had kept a whole troop of men and women around him, just to split out some of the work.

Still at the hedgerow, looking across the field, she could just see John—and the men who were converging on him. Insects buzzed around their glowing lantern. John might be able to trick a pair of them, but not so many.

"John, you've got to get out of there," she murmured.

Henry set his jaw. "I will go and show myself. Command them to leave off."

"Can you be sure they will recognize you and not kill you before you have a chance to speak?"

He scowled. "How is it there's so little I'm allowed to

do? I'm meant to be king!"

"What must I do to serve you, Your Grace?" Walter said tiredly. "I can deliver a message, or, or . . ."

"Be quiet," Henry said. "That's all for now."

"Yes, my liege."

Walter seemed to be coming around but still wasn't steady on his feet. That decided it for Mary; John and Eleanor she could trust on their own, at least a little. Henry and Walter, she could not.

"We will take him to the abbey. Then at least you and he will be safe, and I can go help John."

"I will send guards back with you," he said decisively, as if happy to think of some useful thing he could do.

A shout carried up from the river. John had fallen. The dark-cloaked men had run him down, and now they closed in on him.

"He's done for," Walter stated unhelpfully.

"Eleanor!" Henry exclaimed.

Mary looked and gasped to see the girl running up along the hedgerow. "Eleanor, where have you—"

She held out a bow and quiver of arrows and seemed quite smug to have brought them.

"You went to find weapons," Mary stated, disbelieving. Eleanor nodded. The girl hadn't had enough time to get all the way to the Locksley camp and back. She was barely out of breath. Mary took the bow; it hadn't seen much use. The arrows had brown fletching. She didn't recognize them. "Where did you get these?"

Eleanor pointed vaguely back at the barons' camps. Mary closed her eyes a moment and drew a calming breath so that she wouldn't yell. Yelling never did any good with Eleanor.

"You can't just go taking bows and arrows from people," Mary said—softly. Her little sister shrugged, unapologetic.

"Mary—" Henry said.

She could no longer see her brother, hidden behind the wall of attackers. She drew a handful of arrows, planted them in the ground next to her, raised one to the bow. She had never killed. Now she had the thought that she could kill all these men easily. Henry would pardon her, whatever happened, just from sheer high spirits. But she hesitated—was she ready to kill?

She was not, so she aimed carefully, drawing on a spot a foot or so to the left of the lantern, which served as a bright and easy target. Released her arrow on a long, high arc. Picked up the next arrow and fired. The arrows hit the grass in a row behind the attackers, shots meant to startle, to frighten, not to kill.

It worked. Unable to see where the arrows flew from, unwilling to risk their own lives to finish off the boy's, the men scattered.

Her fourth arrow hit the lantern itself. The candle inside burst and sputtered out. One of the men screamed.

"You three wait here." She went to her brother, who was running toward her, collecting arrows as he came.

"You almost shot me!" he yelled, laughing and gasping for breath.

"No, I didn't."

"Where'd you get the bow? Whose arrows are these?"

"You'll have to ask Eleanor."

"We're going to have so much explaining to do."

"First, we run."

The attackers were already regrouping to follow. The arrows had only temporarily startled them.

When they reached Henry, Eleanor, and Walter, Mary risked a look back. Six men came at them from across the field.

"Go, go," she hissed, urging the others before her, steering them away from the hedgerow, down the lane toward the encampments. Witnesses, right now they needed lots of witnesses. They reached the first of the tents, fires, picket lines, and sleeping horses. Now if they could just find a place to hide and rest for a few moments.

She was about to apologize to the king again, but he was grinning. "Was this what it was like for Robin Hood in Sherwood, do you think, when the sheriff's men chased him?"

"I don't know," Mary said. "How frightened are we all?"

"Robin Hood was never frightened, I'm sure of it," the king insisted.

"The stories tend to leave that part out," John said. "Mother talks mostly about the wet and the cold and holding your breath while the sheriff's men walk by and every little noise wracking your nerves. So, yes, I'd say this was a lot like it was for them."

"But we saved Walter's life," Henry insisted. He so wanted to be useful.

"Well, I did promise an adventure," John said tiredly.

Henry spoke carefully. "A king must do great deeds. Everyone knows this. But I'm not sure what I can do."

"You don't have to do great deeds right now," Mary said, trying to sound reassuring. "You're only thirteen. Plenty of time to do great deeds later."

But Henry insisted. "I might reclaim my family's lands in Normandy. Or go on Crusade like my uncle did."

"All very expensive," John said. "The barons will not like it when you start asking them for money for wars abroad."

"Yes, I know. But I am king." As if this explained everything. As if going on Crusade was anything like being an outlaw in Sherwood Forest.

"Perhaps it would be enough for you to be a good *English* king," Mary said.

"Like Edward the Confessor. He was a great man!" Henry said.

Mary, a little taken aback, said, "Some would say there has not been a good English king since Edward, before the Normans came."

"William the Conqueror is my forefather. I am his direct heir. Do you disparage him?"

"No. Forgive me, sire. I'm a bit tired just now."

"Line all my ancestors up—it's a lot to live up to," Henry said. "I don't see how I can."

"Do not worry so, my liege," John said. "Some things take care of themselves."

"I suppose so. But this man would have died if you had done nothing. Some things do not take care of themselves."

"There they are!" a voice called from behind him.

They could not keep running.

Eleanor took hold of Mary's arm and pointed to a camp with lit torches and restless horses. Men still worked setting up tents, as if the company had just arrived.

"Why there?" Mary asked, and Eleanor laid her hand on the bow. "The camp where you got the bow from? Well, we'll have to return it in any case. The folk there seemed friendly to you?"

Eleanor nodded.

"Do we risk it?" John asked.

"We can't keep on like this. We must hide, I think," Mary said, and they ducked off the path, into the edge of the camp.

The missing bow had been noticed. Near the largest of the pavilions, a man was studying a rack, where swords, spears, and bows rested. He counted, counted again, looked around quizzically. Hard to get a good look at him in the near-dark. He seemed young, not much taller than Mary herself but powerfully built.

He noticed the odd company straight off, and his hand went to the sword on his belt. Fortunately, it stayed there. He stood with a bearing that suggested he was used to being listened to. Well born—a knight, even, given the sword. Not used to having weapons stolen from his camp.

She held up the bow and quiver. "I'm very sorry to bother you, sir. I've come to return this. And to ask for help. We're in a bit of trouble." All of them were breathing hard from the running, and Walter was clearly injured. She tried to seem harmless and contrite but was afraid she merely looked crazed. "We just need a place to hide for a bit."

He glanced down the path where they'd come. Their

pursuers had split up, and a pair of them approached, on the hunt.

"My lady, of course. This way." He gathered the weapons from her and herded them around to the back of the tent. Once hidden, they stood still, breaths held. Mary's chest hurt from holding it. She touched Eleanor's shoulder, made sure Walter stayed upright, and didn't have a hand left for anything else. The young knight kept watch.

Voices approached.

"They've gone this way!" one of the men called.

"I don't see them anymore."

"We must find that wretched boy—"

They carried on, out of hearing.

The young man nodded, satisfied. "I think they've gone for now."

They all sighed. Mary rubbed her face and muttered, "God."

"Now, please, tell me what's happened—Your Grace!" He noticed Henry and bowed low.

Everyone had that exact same reaction. It was almost laughable, this man deferring to the lanky boy.

"Thank you for your help, sir," Henry said solemnly.

"Then you all aren't kidnapping the king?" the man asked.

"No!" Mary said, horrified, with more vehemence than was probably necessary.

John said, "We think those men are mounting some conspiracy against the Bishop of Winchester. They meant to drown Walter, and if they placed some incriminating evidence with him—"

"He would seem to be a spy," the young man added, nodding with understanding.

Henry's gaze narrowed. "If the blame fell on Lord Peter, it might be enough to throw him out of power."

"And who are all of you?"

Mary had been about to answer when Henry said, "They are our friends." Which kept their names out of it, which might have been for the best. She pressed her lips together, quiet as Eleanor. The king added, "We need to return to the palace without being seen. Can you help us?"

"I can loan you horses," he said. "Your enemies are looking for a group on foot. Horses will get you back faster, and they won't suspect you."

"That's a good idea," John said. "Thank you."

They waited a bit longer, to give their pursuers more time to move on. Their host gave them a little wine to drink, and they sat silently with their worn nerves. Finally, Mary had had enough of the man looking them over and politely not asking any questions. He was being so very kind, and she was grateful. But the night was wearing on.

"Your Grace, we should go," she said. "Get you home before anyone notices you're gone."

"I imagine they've already noticed," Henry said. He seemed pleased about it. "Be easy, my lady. There'll be no trouble. I'll make sure of it."

The young knight brought them to his picket line of horses. In the middle of the camp, there was more torchlight, and Mary got a better look at him. He was in his twenties and definitely well born. His tunic was finely made, embroidered on the edges. He had a neat beard and a ready smile. Handsome. She looked away.

He paused between a pair of good-looking palfreys, one gray and one brown. "These two, I think. One for your injured clerk, one for His Grace. We can move quickly with little notice. Albert, get them saddled, please," he called to an hostler.

"You'll come with us?" Mary asked, sounding far too eager.

"I think I must, to see no harm comes to you all."

He rubbed the brown mare between her eyes, and the horse reached for him. "There, Daisy. Sorry to wake you up, but we've important work to do. Here now, be patient!" The mare Daisy stretched her nose to the pouch on his belt, *wuffing* through her nose, lips grasping, and he laughed. Sure enough, he drew out a couple of bits of carrot from the pouch. Daisy had known they were there.

He also gave the gray horse a couple of treats and rubbed his ears. Mary was enthralled. She *liked* this man . . . but she was tired and not thinking straight and decided she should not think of him at all.

Soon enough, the wayward party was on the path leading out of the camp and to the main way to Westminster. The kind knight led the horse that carried Walter; the Locksley siblings walked alongside King Henry's mount, Daisy. They needed to be off quickly before their pursuers returned.

"Thank you for your help, my lord," Mary said tiredly.

"My true pleasure, my lady."

John was the one who finally asked, "My lord, what is your name, so we know who has our gratitude."

"Sir William de Ros, of Helmsley Castle."

The world froze for a heartbeat. Mary thought she might faint. Or scream, only that would startle the horses. She thought of running away, but then the name burst out of her with a complete lack of propriety. "William de Ros!"

And yes, the horses startled at the exclamation, but only a little. They were very well trained.

He regarded her, brow furrowed. "Um, yes?"

"But I've been trying to meet you for *years*!"

"You have?" Even more confused.

They stared at one another. She had no idea what to

say next. Neither did he, evidently.

"You will have to tell him who you are," John whispered.

Yes, right. She shook her head, trying to clear the muzziness that suddenly filled her. "I'm Mary of Locksley."

The man brightened, smiled wide. "You are?"

Then they were both staring again, silent, tongue-tied. He must think her stupid.

"What's happening?" Henry whispered.

John explained. "These two have been betrothed—well, mostly betrothed—for *ages*. But between wars and invasions and—"

It was all too much. Mary still wanted to run away, but she did not think her legs would work just now. "And then you went to the continent to fight in tournaments for a year." She sounded shrill. She was going mad. *His horses like him* . . . "Were you trying to avoid me?"

"My lady, no, of course not—"

"Are you any good?" Henry interrupted. "At the tournaments, I mean."

"I had some success, yes," William said, a bit smugly, Mary thought. She suddenly wanted to see him ride. To see if he had calluses on his hands from fighting. To see how strong he really was. She bit her lip. "My lady, it's only that I thought if I wanted to test my mettle, I ought to go before I married rather than after."

"Well, yes, but . . ." She caught her breath, her eyes watered, she rubbed her face and turned away—"And finally, here we are, and look at me, I'm a *mess*, in my worst kirtle, without a veil, covered in dirt and sweat, what you must think of me—"

Eleanor stepped up, put her hand on Mary's mouth and glared with an admonishing look. Mary subsided.

William de Ros, who had been William de Ros this entire time and she didn't even know it, bowed graciously. "Lady Mary. You are very well met."

"I am?"

"I think meeting you like this is better than in some hall with God and everybody looking on."

"Oh. I . . ." She had lost all sense and power of speech. This was stupid. She ought to say something clever and gracious.

"You there! Where are you going!" A group of dark-cloaked men approached from behind. Two of them had swords. They quickened their paces.

"Oh, no," Mary murmured.

"You go on ahead," William said. "I'll take care of this."

"Are you sure—"

"All I need to do is delay them. Go now."

Mary still wasn't entirely sure William de Ros existed. She didn't want to go, but the horses had become nervous, not to mention the people around them. "Can I see you tomorrow?" she blurted.

"I will come and see you tomorrow," he said.

"You promise?"

"On my honor I promise. Now go!"

"Mary, come on!" John urged her. He took hold of the reins of Walter's horse while William jogged on to intercept their pursuers.

Mary, John, and Eleanor went quickly, hurrying the horses. Behind them, William stood in the middle of the track, hands on hips, taking up space.

"Good sirs, you seem to be in some distress. Is there anything I can help you with?" he announced cheerfully.

"No, my lord; if you will step aside—"

"But if you'll just tell me what the matter is—"

By then, Mary and the others were out of earshot. She kept them moving, toward the beacon of the towering abbey.

"I like him," Henry announced after they had ridden a ways. "I think you should marry him."

Mary didn't want to think about that just now. "Is that a royal command, sire?" And what would she do if he said yes?

"Only a suggestion," he said.

They walked on. This night could not finish soon enough.

~

The palace courtyard was in an uproar, blazing with torches and a whole troop of horses waiting to set off. Guards and clerks swarmed, and on the low steps leading up to the hall a cluster of serious men were in conference. The young king's absence had been noted.

John sighed. His plan for returning depended on no one noticing Henry was gone. "We'll never get past all this."

"We will all *hang*," Mary said, disgusted.

"His Grace won't," Walter added helpfully.

They stayed back on the road, where they could lurk unnoticed for the time being. "Perhaps if we go around back," John murmured, calculating. They could pretend they were serving boys. Except *everyone* recognized Henry . . .

The king swung off his horse. "Never mind. I'll take care of this. Walter, can you walk?"

"Yes, sire." The clerk slid down more cautiously, and wonder of wonders, once on the ground, he stayed upright.

"Lord John, follow my lead," Henry said. "Whatever anyone asks, tell them I ordered you." John blinked at the king, nonplussed. Maybe the boy knew what he was about after all. Henry then turned to Mary. "Lady Mary, you and your sister must keep out of this mess."

"Not at all," Mary said vehemently. "I've got to keep you lot out of trouble—"

John looked at her. "He's right. Whatever happens, it's best if you aren't tangled up in it. You should wait here with the horses."

The implication was clear, even if his sister didn't want to admit it: the ladies had their reputations to think of. Mary locked her mouth shut and glared. She took one set of reins, Eleanor the other.

"Lady Mary, Lady Eleanor—thank you. I hope to see you again soon." King Henry beamed at them. Well, at least someone had had fun this night. The sisters bowed in return.

"I'll be back in a moment, once we've cleared this up," John assured her, and hoped it was true.

On foot then, like vagrants, the king, the clerk, and young lord entered the courtyard. It didn't take long for them to be noticed.

"Sire!" one guard exclaimed, then all fell silent and every face turned to them. At Henry's right shoulder, John held himself straight through an act of will. At the king's left, Walter wilted but kept his feet at least.

Chin up, imperious, King Henry III marched to the palace doors, where the Bishop of Winchester, the Chief Justiciar, the Archbishop of Canterbury, and a half dozen of the most powerful men in the kingdom waited. If John thought about it too much, he would be horrified, but he kept his gaze on Henry. He'd made his oath to the king, not these men. And Henry actually seemed to know what he was doing.

"My lords," Henry said. "What's all this?"

After a nervous conference between the councilors, made with glances and frowns, Peter des Roches was the one who stepped forward. "Your Grace! You . . . you were missing."

"Yes. We had business. But we were well protected." He glanced at John, who tried very hard to look like someone who could protect the king on the road, at night, single-handed.

"Your Grace, I must protest—"

"We met one of your clerks on the way," Henry continued. "He was set upon by attackers, right here in Westminster."

The Bishop of Winchester stared as if poleaxed.

"My lord bishop," Walter murmured apologetically, keeping his gaze on the ground.

"He nearly died," Henry added ominously.

Des Roches studied them. Walter had begun to sway again. "Walter, perhaps you should go to the abbey's infirmary to be looked at."

"Thank you, my lord," Walter said, and managed one more bow to the king before fleeing.

Hubert de Burgh appeared to collect himself in the face of a situation he probably was not expecting and stepped ahead of the bishop to take control. "Your Grace, if there are outlaws abroad, you should have immediately summoned help."

"We are not sure this is a case of outlaws so much as politics," Henry said.

Meanwhile, John had time to scan the courtyard, which had enough shadows for a group of dark-cloaked men to hide in. He had worked hard to note them, to mark what features he could in case he might find them again. And . . . there, standing by a brazier, the original three who'd dragged off Walter. They were burning a letter.

"There they are, Your Grace," he said to Henry, but the others heard, and everyone looked.

The king said, "Lord Justiciar, we heard tell of a letter that was meant to incriminate certain of our servants. Would you have any idea what such a letter might say?"

De Burgh, his expression steady, glanced at his men, one of whom was stamping out the last ashes of the burned page. John watched de Burgh for the least flicker of a reaction, and stood behind his liege lord as if behind a shield.

The Chief Justiciar glanced briefly at the Bishop of Winchester and nodded to the king. "I don't know what letter you speak of, Your Grace."

"Indeed," Henry said calmly.

In the meantime, Peter des Roches was turning florid. "Your Grace, it is very late. Perhaps you would like to return to your chambers?"

For a moment, John thought Henry was going to refuse, out of high spirits or a need to continue wielding this authority he'd discovered. But it *was* very late, and the young king seemed suddenly tired. His shoulders slouched, just a little.

"Very well," Henry said. He turned to John. "Thank you for your good service to us, Lord John. You may go."

"I am always your servant, Your Grace." John bowed deeply, glancing up long enough to see Henry smile before he turned to the door and went inside, flanked by actual guards.

And that was the end of that.

John straightened and started to turn, when both de Burgh and des Roches were suddenly before him. *This is it,* John thought. *Now I am done for.*

"My lord Justiciar. We will have words later," des Roches stated calmly, but his glare was iron.

De Burgh looked as if he thought to say one thing, then smiled wryly. "We always do, my lord bishop." He turned and walked off. The men, John's attackers from earlier in the evening, started to scurry after the Chief Justiciar, but he angrily waved them off.

"John of Locksley." The Bishop of Winchester said the name like a curse.

"My lord."

"I suppose you expect some sort of show of gratitude."

"Not at all, my lord. Walking out of here on my own two feet is reward enough, I assure you." Now, he must leave here, quickly, before anybody got any ideas about him . . .

"You have an interest in politics?"

"No, my lord. We were just climbing trees."

The bishop tilted his head and seemed confused. "Climbing trees?"

"Yes, my lord."

"Was this your father's idea?"

"Oh, no," John said, determined to leave Robin out of it. "In fact, I think I am going to be in a great deal of trouble the next time I see him. My lord." He winced.

The Bishop of Winchester smiled, snake-like. "Well, then, you'd best be off and get it over with."

"My lord." John bowed himself out, under the intense watch of guards and hostlers and squires and hangers-on. If they could pull him apart with just their stares, they would have.

As soon as he was out of the courtyard and out of sight, he ran.

~

Mary wanted to crawl into bed and sleep for the rest of the day. Dawn was nigh; a half-awake gray haze had crept over them without her noticing. Even the horses' feet were dragging as they finally returned home. All she could think: William would have to come see her, if he wanted to get his horses back.

They halted just outside the camp. Robin and his whole company were gathered there and seemed to be preparing for an expedition—quivers over shoulders, swords at hips, bows and staves in hand. Robin, Will Scarlet, Dav of Doncaster, Grace, the rest of their troop, Marian with a cloak over her shoulders, lantern in hand. There'd be no sneaking past this.

"Damn," John muttered.

Their father put his hands on his hips as he looked them up and down. "Well. Good morning, my darling children."

"Morning, sir!" John said brightly as if they had just come back from picking berries. "You're all up early!"

They spent what seemed a very long time, the returning party and the would-be departing party, regarding one another.

"So, no rescue needed?" Robin finally asked.

Mary had no idea how to answer that.

"What's he doing here?" John exclaimed, looking past the company to a spot by the fire. A staff had been driven into the ground, and a man was sitting there tied to it with ropes around his arms and legs, a gag in his mouth and tears running down his face and into his beard.

"Ranulf FitzHugh," she said coldly. What had he done now?

"Ah, yes, Lord Ranulf is enjoying some of the old traditional Sherwood hospitality," Robin said merrily, but his gaze was steel.

Marian's look had an edge to it as well, reminding them that she had grown up amidst the cutthroat rivalries of the Norman court. No one could underestimate her when she was like this. "Dav and Grace caught him sneaking around back. He said there was a matter of honor he intended to talk to you two about. I'm sure I don't know what he means."

"I'd rather swim to France than talk to him," Mary said. What had the man intended? Her thoughts would not dwell on the question.

Robin said, "We still haven't quite decided what to do with him."

It seemed like rather a lot had been done with him already. The man didn't have a mark on him, but his face was drawn with a look of fear and anguish. And what idiot decided it was a good idea to try to sneak into Locksley's camp?

"Put him in the river," John said, glaring. "Give him a cooling-off."

"An awfully long walk to the river," Grace said.

Will answered, "Set him backward on one of the horses and see how long he stays on—"

The talk went on like this, back and forth, and Mary's patience ended abruptly. She couldn't listen to another word, the night had already lasted far longer than it should have, and none of this was funny.

"Hold this," Mary said, handing Daisy's reins to John. She went to the rack of weapons by the main tent and fetched a bow and quiver. Strung it right there, where Ranulf was tied up and the rest of them were bantering. The laughter faded until all stared at her.

"Father," she said. "Set him loose. Make him run. I'll show him how well I shoot at a moving target." She chose an arrow.

Robin hesitated, glancing at Ranulf, returning his gaze to his daughter, and she wondered what her father saw in her eyes. Robin's smile fell.

It was Marian who finally spoke. "Do it."

For a moment, Mary thought Robin would refuse. Maybe he ought to have refused. But he looked at his wife, his daughter, and nodded.

"As my lady commands. Dav, set him loose," Robin said, and Dav drew a knife and cut the ropes.

Ranulf scrambled to hands and knees, looking around wildly. His hands came together, as if he meant to beg at Robin's feet. He looked at Mary and her bow, and his eyes grew wide.

"You'd better run," the baron of Locksley said. "I'm not going to stop her."

Mary nocked her arrow.

With a choked cry, Ranulf ran, out of the camp, straight across the field. He glanced back once. Mary drew the string to her chin. He ran on, managing to go even faster.

Sighing, she lowered the bow and let out the tension. And that was that.

Robin blew out a breath and put a hand on her shoulder. She smiled weakly.

The rigid silence of all who had been watching broke. Dav and Grace bent over each other's shoulders, laughing hard, along with the rest of Robin's troop. Will Scarlet continued watching the fleeing Ranulf and seemed very satisfied.

"Did you see the look on his face?" John asked wonderingly.

"I only saw the back of him," Dav said, laughing.

Marian turned on the children. "Now, where have

you been all night!"

Mary still didn't have a good answer for that. At least she had the excuse of unstringing the bow and putting away arrows rather than looking at her mother. Eleanor answered for them: she simply marched past them, making a broad gesture that was surprisingly eloquent in dismissing all of them and their nonsense.

Marian turned to the next in line. "John?"

John heaved a sigh. "Court politics is stupid," he said, handed the reins of both horses to Mary, and followed Eleanor away.

Leaving Mary to offer any further explanations. They were all looking at her expectantly. "It might be better if you didn't know," she said finally.

"Really, Mary," Robin said. "I would like to know."

"Where did you get those horses?" Will Scarlet interrupted.

She worked to keep her voice steady. "From Sir William de Ros of Helmsley Castle." She would never be able to explain, not in a thousand years.

"William de Ros!" Robin exclaimed.

"Yes, he is coming to see us tomorrow. Today, rather." She looked skyward. Yes, it was today.

"You met William?" Marian said. "In the middle of the night, unchaperoned, doing God knows what—"

"Will, could you help me picket these two until Sir

William comes for them?" Mary asked tiredly.

"Yes, of course."

She handed the horses to the care of Will and his assistant, which gave her leave to try to get at least a little sleep before William arrived.

Astonished, her parents both said, together, "Mary!"

Mary continued through the camp, pausing to add over her shoulder, "I like him."

~

William arrived late that morning. Everyone made excuses to come and get a look at him, except for Mary, who was in the back of the tent in a panic. Her mother tried to calm her.

"I must look terrible, my eyes must be bloodshot, and I'm sure my veil isn't straight—"

"You are beautiful, my child." Marian held her face and kissed her on the forehead. Mary couldn't breathe before, but the touch settled her. "Now come be sociable."

Her mother brought her to the camp's forecourt, and had to give her only a little push to make her step forward, to her father's side.

"My daughter, Lady Mary," Robin announced to Sir William, standing properly before them. He looked very well in the daylight, which brought out golden hints in his light-brown hair, and his smile lit his eyes, which were blue. She hadn't noticed the color of his eyes in the dark. He was neatly turned out in an embroidered coat, his sword at his side.

It was suggested that she and William go for a walk together, just around the meadow and back. So they did, side by side, with a polite space between them. All very proper.

Mary decided that William was right: she preferred the way they met, in a panic without worrying about saying the wrong thing.

"I hope you didn't have too much trouble keeping those men off us," she said in a rush, when they were out of earshot of camp. "I really hadn't meant for you to get involved." Mary took an extra look around, sure that John and Eleanor were creeping around trying to eavesdrop. She didn't see them. Perhaps Mother had tied them to a bench.

"It was no trouble. By the time they got past me, you all were well away. I'm happy you all got back safely," he said.

"We had a bit of trouble at the palace, but the king cut straight through it."

"What good is being king if you can't smooth out trouble?"

"Thank you for loaning us the horses. We'd never have got everyone through safely without you."

"You're very welcome. I like a bit of adventure."

"Well, yes, it's all right for you, a knight who is used to fighting—"

"Are you the one who fired those arrows?" he asked, his smile crooked. "They had dirt and grass stuck to the heads. Someone fired them. No blood, at least."

"No, thank God," she admitted. "I just needed to drive them off, not kill anyone."

"Ah. So, you're pretty handy with a bow."

Of course I am, I am Robin Hood's daughter . . . "After last night, you must think me awful and wild and un-womanly and . . ." She ran out of descriptions.

"I think you're . . . intriguing."

"Intriguing." She smiled wryly. "Like a strange horse that's just turned up."

They had gotten quite far from camp now, and part of her wanted to run back home, all the way to Sherwood, this was too much, he was smiling, and she couldn't tell if he was pleased or laughing at her, if looking her over in daylight made her seem better or worse than she had during last night's adventure. She couldn't tell what he was thinking; she did not know him.

And she wanted to hold his hand, and more.

He stopped, turned to her so they stood face to face, and said, "Last night, I thought, this is a woman I could tell to bar the doors of the castle, and no one would ever get through. That is the kind of woman I would like to marry. If you'll have me."

She had the feeling of stepping off the edge of a cliff as she said, "I will. Yes."

He offered his hand. She lay hers in it, and he kissed it lightly, just a brush of lips on her knuckles. Then, her hand still resting in his, they returned to the Locksley camp.

～

That same morning, shortly before the long-awaited arrival of Sir William de Ros, John of Locksley received a letter stamped with the royal seal. He read it and turned pensive.

Then Sir William arrived and all was chaos, and Marian threatened him and Eleanor with a whole litany of curses if they tried to sneak out to spy on the couple on their walk, but John wasn't so interested as he might have been.

Well, he was interested, and that was a problem.

"What's this, then?" Robin asked him when the pair had gone off and everyone needed distracting to not stare after them like they were watching acrobats. *Dancing bears,* Mary had complained.

John showed him the letter. "The king has asked me to

Carrie Vaughn

stay and be part of his court. To teach him archery."

Robin smiled wide. "Well done, John."

"Is this what you wanted?" he asked, accusing. "To throw me to that pack of wolves at court to curry favor? That's what des Roches thinks."

His father paced, squinting out at the cluster of buildings that was Westminster. "I wanted better for you. I could never make friends with the kings of England, but if you—" He shook his head, glanced away. "I simply wondered what it must be like to have royal favor rather than be eternally out of it. That is all I wished for you." He sounded wistful.

"What does royal favor matter? Only right and wrong matter. Justice. That's what you always taught us." *What the stories taught,* he almost said. Nevertheless, Robin understood what remained unspoken.

"Yes. But you must realize that a man often behaves quite differently after he has children than he did before."

John's anger faded. "I begin to understand why Little John stayed in the greenwood all those years."

"There were times I thought I should have followed him. Well, you can't ignore a royal summons. Or you can, but that has . . . implications." Robin winked.

"But what is one to do with men like Peter des Roches and Hubert de Burgh? All the other bishops and lords around him? They'll never leave me alone. You should

118

see the sour looks they get whenever they hear the name Locksley."

His father had the grace to look a little chagrined at that. Then he said, "Ignore them. Well, that's not exactly right. More like, you don't react to them. They will suspect you, try to manipulate you, put you out of favor as much as they can. They will be jealous of you, if the king turns to you for any kind of advice, even if he only ever speaks to you of the weather. And you—well, you're simply there to teach the king archery, aren't you?"

Sir William and his sister were still walking, still talking. They seemed very intent on one another.

"I suppose I will have to find a wife soon," he said.

"Plenty of time for that. Then again, perhaps not. Time does seem to be passing more and more quickly." Robin gave his shoulder a companionable pat and went back to see to Marian, who was wringing her hands and almost but not quite crying. She would take it very hard when Mary went away.

They could just see Mary and Sir William at the other end of the field. They all saw him raise her hand to his lips, saw her draw just that little bit closer. So, that was going well, at least.

At least Father hadn't said anything about producing an heir. That seemed a very distant thing, a song sung in a foreign language. On the other hand, when John watched

William de Ros—then, he felt something, some stirring that he didn't want to think of, and so he locked it away. Or tried to.

That man was very handsome.

Scowling, John walked away from camp and kept walking until he'd been through the copse of trees and back and felt no more such stirrings.

When he returned, Sir William had gone, taking his horses with him, and Mary was sitting on the bench by the fire. Eleanor sat beside her with her spindle. Both it and her fingers seemed to blur, she worked so fast, which meant she was anxious. She stared hard at the thread she was making.

John came and settled on Mary's other side.

"That seemed to go well," John said.

"It did. I think our fathers have decided on a week from Sunday for the wedding."

He stared. "So soon!"

"We've been waiting four years." She shrugged. "I'd rather it come sooner than later, if it's going to come at all."

Eleanor spun faster until the thread broke. She heaved a sigh, retrieved the dropped spindle, and spliced the broken thread back with the roving.

"What made you decide?" John asked.

She laughed softly. "His horses like him. Is that silly?"

"No, not at all. And you'll go away with him to York-shire?"

"I suppose so, yes."

He stared at the fire, which was only a few flames licking at a single log nestled among embers. Someone ought to build it back up soon. There wasn't much smoke coming up from it, but nonetheless, his eyes stung.

"What will I ever do without you?" he said finally.

She wouldn't look at him but took his hand and squeezed hard. Her eyes shone with unshed tears, locked away by force of will. "I will miss you both so much," she whispered.

Eleanor dropped the spindle and lay her head in her sister's lap. John put his hand on Eleanor's head, held Mary's hand, and they sat like that for a long time.

"We'll all visit each other," Mary said finally, scrubbing her face, straightening. Proper, practical Mary. "Think of all the stories we'll have to tell. You must both collect stories to tell me. Even you, Eleanor." Eleanor smiled. "We will visit each other as often as we can, and we will manage."

"Yes," John said, but he had never felt so sad. "We will."

Author's Note

Every novel about Robin Hood from the last forty years or so ends with an author's note discussing the difficulty of writing about a historical Robin Hood, and justifying the choices the authors made in portraying their own versions. The man likely didn't exist, all the bits that have accrued to the myth over the course of the six hundred years since the first stories were written down are horribly anachronistic, and how is an author to manage? (Did you know that the term "friar" refers specifically to members of the Franciscan and Dominican orders, which did not arrive in England until the early 1220s, five or so years after the death of King John, which means that you *cannot* have Friar Tuck and Prince John in England at the same time and be historically accurate? Now you know!)

Well, I'm not going to write that note because I'm not sure any of that really matters. Because all Robin Hood stories are fanfiction. Robin Hood started out as fanfiction and has never been anything else. The very first written Robin Hood stories from the fifteenth century were likely compilations from oral tradition—favorite bits and pieces that the author arranged in a manner of their liking. For six hundred years now, authors have decided they like these characters and set out to put their own spin on the story. To tell the story *their* way. Fanfiction.

I'm not going to write a long note justifying the choices I made in portraying certain details about the various legends and the various possible historical iterations of said legends. What's more important, I think, is asking a lot of questions about why we're still telling Robin Hood stories at all. What is it we're responding to? What do we want to see in them? What makes a good Robin Hood story?

Adventure. Charm. Good people we like looking out for each other—it's not enough to have a story about Robin Hood. He needs all his friends around him, and they need to be witty and skilled and admirable. Archery, of course we need archery. Clint Barton and Katniss Everdeen insist that we still need archery even in this modern day. And Robin needs to help people. He needs to denounce corruption and tyranny. He rebels and resists.

We will never see the end of Robin Hood. We'll keep seeing these stories forever, because they distill so much of what good stories are supposed to do. I do very much think we need Robin Hood stories right now, more than ever.

A couple of thank-yous: Jeff Womack, my historical

archery guru, read over my drafts and made essential suggestions. All errors remaining are my own. Dr. April Harper, medieval scholar, responded to news that I was writing historical fiction set in the early thirteenth century by immediately mailing me the books I needed for research. My agent, Seth Fishman, for the encouragement, my editor Lee Harris for "getting it," and the whole crew at Tor.com Publishing. And always, my friends and family for keeping me on a somewhat even keel.

About the Author

Photograph by Helen Sittig

CARRIE VAUGHN'S work includes the Philip K. Dick Award–winning novel *Bannerless,* the *New York Times* bestselling Kitty Norville urban fantasy series, and over twenty novels and upwards of one hundred short stories, two of which have been finalists for the Hugo Award. Her most recent work includes a Kitty spinoff collection, *The Immortal Conquistador.* She's a contributor to the Wild Cards series of shared-world superhero books edited by George R. R. Martin and a graduate of the Odyssey Writing Workshop. An Air Force brat, she survived her nomadic childhood and managed to put down roots in Boulder, Colorado. Visit her at www.carrievaughn.com.

TOR·COM

Science fiction. Fantasy. The universe.

And related subjects.

*

More than just a publisher's website, *Tor.com*
is a venue for **original fiction, comics,** and
discussion of the entire field of SF and fantasy,
in all media and from all sources. Visit our site
today—and join the conversation yourself.